A Story

by G. Sofer

translated by
Shaindel Weinbach

illustrated by
Miriam Bardugo

A Day

Stories from our history and heritage,
from ancient times to modern times,
arranged according to the Jewish calendar.

Published by

Mesorah Publications, ltd

in conjunction with

SAPIR /
Jerusalem

FIRST EDITION
First Impression . . . January, 1989

Published and Distributed by
MESORAH PUBLICATIONS, Ltd.
Brooklyn, New York 11232
in conjunction with
SAPIR / *Jerusalem*

Distributed in Israel by
MESORAH MAFITZIM / J. GROSSMAN
Rechov Harav Uziel 117
Jerusalem, Israel

Distributed in Europe by
J. LEHMANN HEBREW BOOKSELLERS
20 Cambridge Terrace
Gateshead, Tyne and Wear
England NE8 1RP

THE ARTSCROLL YOUTH SERIES®
A STORY A DAY III: Shevat-Adar
© *Copyright 1988, by* MESORAH PUBLICATIONS, Ltd.
4401 Second Avenue / Brooklyn, N.Y. 11232 / (718) 921-9000

ISBN:
0-89906-954-1 (hard cover)
0-89906-955-X (paperback)

Typography by CompuScribe at ArtScroll Studios, Ltd.
4401 Second Avenue / Brooklyn, N.Y. 11232 / (718) 921-9000

Printed in the United States of America by Noble Book Press Corp.
Bound by Sefercraft, Quality Bookbinders, Ltd. Brooklyn, N.Y.

ᴇᔥ Table of Contents

Shevat

Adar

Shevat

On this day Moshe *Rabbenu* began reviewing and explaining the Torah to the Israelites before his death. He taught them until his last day on this world, the seventh of *Adar* And, like the generation which received the Torah — so has each succeeding generation of Jews yearned to study and know the Torah.

The Answer to the Question

The renowned R' Moshe Shick was born on the 21st of *Adar*, 5567 (1807), and passed away on the first of *Shevat*, 5639 (1879). When his daughter reached marriageable age, he went to seek a suitable husband for her. He traveled from one *yeshivah* to another and in each one, would select the best students and pose a difficult question before them. "Whoever can give me the answer to my question will become my daughter's *chasan*," he would announce each time.

Who would not want the honor of becoming the son-in-law of the famous Maharam Shick? Small wonder, then, that the young students wracked their brains to find the answer to his question. They argued back and forth, analyzed the question from all sides and built towers of discourse, but all in vain. It was so complex that no one succeeded in answering it.

The Maharam Shick

The Maharam Shick did not despair. He carried on with his search for the ideal son-in-law, going from *yeshivah* to *yeshivah*, putting forth the problem in each one. Wherever he went, the students eagerly grappled with the question, but no one could find a satisfactory solution.

At one of the *yeshivos* R' Moshe saw that, as usual, no one was able to solve his problem. He entered his carriage and began the long journey home. The horses turned into the main highway and had begun galloping at full speed when, suddenly, a cry split the air. "Wait! *Rebbe!* Stop! Wait!"

It was not easy to check the horses after they had already gained momentum, but he finally succeeded in bringing them to a halt. Looking behind, R' Moshe saw one of the students racing towards him, puffing and panting with exertion.

As soon as he was within earshot, the young man gasped out, "The question ... the rabbi's question ..."

R' Moshe's eyes opened wide. "Have you found an answer to it?" he asked in surprise.

The boy lowered his gaze in embarrassment. "No. That is beyond my capacity. I could not answer such a difficult question. But ... ," he hesitated, "I wanted to know the answer."

"But I said that the one who knew the answer would become my son-in-law," R' Moshe reminded him.

The youth nodded. "I know. But even if I cannot marry your daughter, does that mean that I can never know the answer to your difficult question?"

The Maharam beamed at the young man with pleasure. "Aha! You are the very one I am looking for! You are fit to become my son-in-law! When I presented my complex question to the students, I was certain that no one would produce the answer. And yet, I was looking for the young man who was interested in the answer, despite the fact that he would not receive the reward attached to it. I sought a young man who was troubled enough by the question to seek the answer, no matter what!"

On this day in 5560 (1800), R' Zusha of Anipoli passed away. R' Zusha was known as a worker of miracles and an outstanding *tzaddik*. He was one of the shining figures of the Chasidic movement.

A Written Guarantee

One year before R' Dov Ber, the *Maggid* of Mezeritch, passed away, a terrible epidemic gripped his city, claiming victim after victim.

The government decided to quarantine Mezeritch. The entire region was to have no contact with the outside world. Whoever broke the quarantine, in any way, was to be put to death.

Anipoli was outside the limits of the afflicted area, but R' Zusha, who was concerned about the health of the *Maggid*, disregarded the law. Somehow, he succeeded in reaching R' Dov Ber in Mezeritch.

"Your life is in danger here," he said to the *Rebbe*. "You must flee as quickly as possible!" He offered his home in Anipoli as a haven for the *Rebbe*.

The *Maggid* agreed to leave the stricken city together with his disciple. After many narrow escapes, they succeeded in reaching Anipoli.

The mayor of Anipoli soon learned about the hidden visitor who had arrived in his city without a permit.

He sent for R' Zusha and said, "You deserve to be put to death for having smuggled a man from the disease-ridden area to our city, which is free of the plague. You have defied the authorities and endangered us all."

R' Zusha replied, "Your anger is fully justified, Your Honor, and your zeal in protecting the residents of our city is to be applauded. It is understandable that you do not want anyone to carry the dread disease and infect the entire population. But, in order to set your mind at rest, I promise that in the year to come no man will die in all of Anipoli."

The mayor had already heard much about R' Zusha's reputation as a saintly man and he respected his word. He agreed to stay the punishment and see if the promise held true. But he demanded a detailed written guarantee stating what had just been said.

R' Zusha complied. He wrote out his promise on a sheet of paper which he duly dated — the nineteenth of *Kislev*, 5631 (1871) — and affixed his signature.

And lo! The *tzaddik*'s promise was borne out in full. During that entire year not a single person died in the city of Anipoli!

When the year had come full circle and it was again the nineteenth of *Kislev* of 5632 (1872), the *Maggid* of Mezeritch was summoned to Heaven, old and sated with years. And indeed, he is buried in Anipoli to this very day!

Rabbi Zilberstein, the last rabbi of Mezeritch, would tell this story. He, himself, had seen the letter which R' Zusha wrote for the mayor and which the Jewish community preserved in its records.

"I also visited the cemetery of Anipoli," the rabbi would add, "and examined all of the tombstones. Indeed, not one bears a date between the nineteenth of *Kislev* of 5631 (1871) and the nineteenth of *Kislev* of the following year."

On the evening of this day, that is, on the eve of the fourth of *Shevat*, R' Yisrael Abuchatzera, known as the "Baba Sali", passed away. R' Yisrael was a most saintly *tzaddik* who performed wonders of salvation for his people. Born on *Rosh Hashanah* of 5650 (1890), he died in 5744 (1984) and was buried in Netivot, the town in southern Israel where he lived and toiled. His grave has become a prayer shrine for thousands of Jews.

Respect for the Torah

R' Yisrael Abuchatzera's star first shone forth in Morocco. When he went up to *Eretz Yisrael*, it continued to shine in the town of Yavne.

Then, suddenly, one day, R' Yisrael called his family together and announced, "We must leave Yavne at once and move elsewhere. I cannot live here any longer!"

The family, which had already become accustomed to Yavne, was not eager to tear up its roots and settle in a different town. They begged R' Yisrael to reconsider or, at least, to postpone the move.

But the *tzaddik* was adamant. That very day he gathered all of his belongings and moved to Ashkelon, where his son lived. From there he went to settle, permanently, in Netivot.

The cause for the sudden move soon became known. One

R' Yisrael Abuchatzera

of the communal figures of Yavne happened to be an erudite
scholar who rejoiced at the *tzaddik*'s dwelling there and
became a fervent admirer of his. He would visit R' Yisrael's
home frequently to 'speak in learning' or to seek advice on
communal matters. Whenever he came, he invariably begged
the *tzaddik*'s blessing for himself and for the community.

In the course of one of these visits, he touched upon the
subject of the studies in the local *yeshivah*, noting the
difference between the approach of the Gaon of Vilna and
that of R' Yisrael Baal Shem Tov. "R' Eliyahu of Vilna studied
in depth," he said, "while the Baal Shem Tov was superficial."

R' Yisrael heard this and winced with pain. But out of deference to his guest, he did not say a word.

As soon as the man had left the house, however, he rose and declared, "It is forbidden to live in a place where they speak disrespectfully of the holiest of holies, the saintly Baal Shem Tov!"

His family tried to calm him, but he refused to be mollified. He sat there and repeated, "It is forbidden to live in a place where they speak disrespectfully of the Baal Shem Tov!"

Within a few hours, he was out of Yavne, never to return.

The Secret of the Puddle

*I*n the evenings, towards midnight, R' Yisrael Abuchatzera would rise to mourn over the *Beis Hamikdash*. He would sit on the ground and pray with deep feeling and emotion, weeping over the exile of the *Shechinah* and the difficult state of his people. During this time, he would shut his door and forbid anyone to enter.

Upon completing his prayer, he appeared utterly exhausted, as if after an unbearable effort.

"Once," his wife told, "I was busy with household chores and forgot all about the hour and that the *rav* was now reciting the *tikkun chatzos*. Without realizing what I was doing, I entered his room and saw him seated on the floor, his head bowed to the ground and beside him — a puddle of water. Thinking that something had spilled, I was about to clean it up when the *tzaddik* raised his head and said, 'I have requested that no one enter my room during this time. But since you entered and saw what you saw, I ask you not to reveal it to anyone.' The water which I saw on the floor, I then realized, was the tears which the holy man had shed over the suffering of his people, the tribulations of the *galus*."

The *rabbanit* kept the secret until her saintly husband passed away.

On this day, in 5567 (1807), R' Moshe Leib of Sassov passed away. R' Moshe Leib, who was born in 5505 (1745), was one of the most prominent figures of the Chasidic movement and known as a most holy man. Of his many sublime qualities, the one which stood out above the rest, was his *ahavas Yisrael*, the fervent love for his fellow Jew.

His Footsteps Left No Trace

Night fell. R' Moshe Leib of Sassov sat in his room studying Torah. He accompanied his study with song and the sweetness of his melody burst forth from his throat, enchanting all chance passersby.

The soul of one particular disciple reverberated with feeling and anticipation when he heard the sound of his master's study. Unknown to R' Moshe Leib, only a few steps away the student was hiding in a corner behind a clothes closet. From this vantage point he was able to follow the Rebbe's actions.

He remained concealed for hours, letting the music of his

master's study sweep over him in waves of bliss. How sweet it was! Sweeter than honey!

Then, suddenly, at the stroke of midnight, the sound stopped. R' Moshe Leib closed the *gemara* on his table and rose swiftly.

The hidden *talmid* watched every move with bated breath. R' Moshe Leib went to the closet and drew out a heavy, fur-lined coat such as gentile peasants wore in winter. After it, came a wide, fur, peasant's hat and, finally, a pair of heavy, black, knee-high boots, suitable for tramping in the snow. The *tzaddik* donned them. He pulled the hat down and the coat lapels up, and wound a long woolen scarf around his face, concealing his beard and *payos*. Before slipping out of the house, he picked up a heavy ax. Thus attired, R' Moshe Leib slipped out the front door and, following stealthily a few steps behind, was the disciple.

"Surely no one will recognize R' Moshe Leib," the young man thought. "Who would believe that such a well-bundled figure carrying an ax would be our famous *Rebbe!* Where can he be going and for what purpose?"

The *Rebbe* made his way to the forest at the edge of the city. R' Moshe Leib seemed to be very familiar with the place. With sure, swift steps, he went up to a tree and began wielding his ax, hewing with all his might.

The *Rebbe* chopping wood! The disciple could hardly believe his eyes.

Soon the *Rebbe* was finished. The tree had been felled and cut into firewood. R' Moshe Leib now took out a coil of rope from his pocket and tied the wood into a bundle. Then, with a practiced motion, he hoisted it onto his shoulder and began walking out of the forest.

The young man, following a few feet behind, saw him turn towards town. "Where can he be going now, dressed as he is?" he thought.

He did not have long to wonder, for the *Rebbe* stopped at a small house at the outskirts of the village. It was a ramshackle cottage, dilapidated and showing signs of neglect and poverty.

R' Moshe Leib broke the stillness of the night with a light knock at the door, and a second knock. Then a weak voice answered from inside, "Come in."

R' Moshe Leib opened the door and strode into the miserable hut. The young man crept up to a window.

Poverty cried out from every niche and cranny. There was hardly any furniture. Several thin forms huddled on the ground. A pile of rags served them as both bed and bedding, above and below. In the far corner lay a woman and her infant, newly born, both thinly dressed and shivering with cold.

"Hello, there!" R' Moshe Leib said heartily. "Would you like to buy some firewood? Brr, it's cold in here."

"I could surely use some," the mother said with a sigh, "but I can't afford it. I have no money."

The *tzaddik*, in his guise of a gentile woodchopper, adapted his accent to the role. "Well," he said, "I am too tired to lug this bundle around any more. I'm leaving it here. Use it and pay me back some other time."

So saying, he untied the bundle, threw a few logs on the hearth and lit a fire. Soon a pleasant warmth was radiating from the crackling flames.

The young man watched with amazement from his place at the window. "Well, now that he has lit the fire, the *Rebbe* will probably be going home," he mused.

But R' Moshe Leib was in no rush. He still had work to do. Going over to the stove, he cooked some cereal and called the hungry children to the table to eat. Only after they had eaten their fill did he leave, reminding them that they could pay him for the wood at a later date.

R' Moshe Leib left the house, with his student still shadowing him. He returned home, slipped out of his farmer's disguise and hid the clothing and the ax in his wardrobe. Then he returned to his study as if nothing unusual had happened. He continued thus until the wee hours of the morning . . .

Many years passed. That disciple became the famous R' Tzvi Hirsch of Zidichov, a leader of hundreds of *chasidim*.

Once, when he was seated with his followers, he revealed the events of that special night when he had glimpsed the secret life of his *Rebbe*, R' Moshe Leib of Sassov.

"It was just as it is written in *Tehillim*," R' Tzvi Hirsch observed in conclusion, " 'Your path is in many waters and your footsteps leave no trace.' How well this applies to my master, R' Moshe Leib, whose love for his fellow Jews was boundless.

On this day in 5665 (1905), R' Yehudah Aryeh Leib, the *Sefas Emes*, passed away. Born on the twenty-ninth of *Nisan* 5607 (1847), he was the *Rebbe* of the Gerrer *chasidim*. Many fabulous stories are told about him. Shepherd of myriads of *chasidim*, he guided and taught every one of them, as if each were an only son.

A Heap Worth One Hundred Rubles

One of the grandsons of the *Sefas Emes* married the daughter of a wealthy Warsaw financier. After the wedding, the young man, Meir, lived near his father-in-law and allowed himself to live in luxurious style, as if he himself were a prosperous business-man. His house was wide open to all and many Gerrer *chasidim* frequented his home.

Meir rapidly sank heavily into debt. When his creditors came knocking at the door, demanding their money, the young man had no choice but to pay them from the dowry.

As this sum was held in trust by his grandfather, he sent a relative to the *Sefas Emes* to ask for a portion of the money.

The *Rebbe* agreed to give his grandson the required sum in

order to repay his debts and made an appointment for the young man to come and fetch the money in person.

The grandson arrived on the designated day and hour. The *Sefas Emes* had him shown into his study. There, on the table, lay a huge pile of pennies. This was the money which his grandfather had prepared for him!

"Meir'ke, my son," said the *Rebbe*, "here is one hundred rubles for you to pay back your debts."

The grandson stood in front of the immense pile, bewildered. What was he supposed to do? How was he expected to gather up this large heap of coins? And how could he pay back his debts with all these pennies?

The young man's confusion did not escape his grandfather's discerning eye. "You are surely surprised at the sight of this tremendous heap of coins," he said. "Think a moment, do you know how much a water-carrier earns by drawing water, hoisting his buckets to his shoulders and dragging them up to the top floor where you live?"

"Yes," replied Meir'ke. "He gets three pennies for his two pails."

"Now figure out how many three-penny payments there are in one hundred rubles. A staggering amount, isn't it? Stop to think, my dear grandson, how many years and how much toil that water-carrier must expend until he earns one hundred rubles, the same hundred rubles lying before you on this table in pennies. And now think how quickly you managed to run through the enormous sum heaped up here . . ."

Fortunate

A young man once came to the *Sefas Emes* to unburden himself of his troubles. "People falsely slander me. They have ruined my reputation," he wept.

"And what is that reputation? How do you regard yourself?" the *tzaddik* asked.

"I consider myself to be like the man in the saying, 'Fortunate is the one who is suspect but is innocent'," he replied.

"If so, you had better change that 'fortunate' for the one in another verse, '*Fortunate* are the ones who stay at home.' For if you cease visiting disreputable places, you can be sure that people will not talk about you behind your back."

Rising for Maariv?

A young man once complained to the *Sefas Emes* that he found it impossible to get up early in the morning.

The *Rebbe* replied, "The *mishnah* refers to those who are up early morning and evening. The choice of words is very puzzling. Rising early in the morning is understandable, but what is meant by 'rising in the evening'? The answer is that if one retires early, then he will have no trouble rising early in the morning."

On this day, in 5543 (1783), R' Chaim of Sanz passed away. One of the most astute scholars of Brodi, he is numbered among the great figures of our people.

Anonymously

R' Chaim of Sanz was preoccupied with two concerns. Even though he belonged to a vastly wealthy family, his business had nothing to do with finance or profits.

For the entire day and much of the night, R' Chaim was preoccupied with the study of Torah. That was one "business". And during his free time he busied himself with his other "business" — charity and acts of *chesed*.

They say that when he was engrossed in study at night, he would place two glasses brimming with water upon his table. He placed his hand in one. He studied until the wee hours of the morning — and if he happened to fall asleep, his hand would drop, tipping over the glass and its contents. The sound of the clinking glass would waken him. He would wash his hands from the water in the second glass and resume his study.

R' Chaim of Sanz was fond of saying: "Why do all the tractates begin with page two rather than page one? To teach us that no matter how much a Jew studies, be it day and night, let him not pride himself, for he still has not even reached the first page. He has yet to start."

☙ ☙ ☙

R' Chaim consecrated much of his time, means and energy to charitable matters. Aside from the huge sums which he gave of his own, he made the rounds of the wealthy people in the city to collect their donations for various communal or individual needs.

R' Chaim never went alone to raise funds. Our Sages (*Bava Basra*) rule that charity must not be collected by a single individual and R' Chaim adhered strictly to this rule. Whenever he set out to raise money for any cause, he was always accompanied by one of the prominent men of the community.

So it was upon the occasion of this story:

R' Chaim and another distinguished man went to collect money for a respected member of the community who had fallen on hard times. A large sum was needed to bail him out of bankruptcy and the two men worked diligently and devotedly to raise the required amount.

In their rounds they reached the home of a wealthy resident. From a man of his position they demanded a large donation — five hundred rubles.

"Is this money to go for a private matter or for a communal need?" the man asked.

"It is for one of our respected congregants who is in desperate need of several thousand rubles," R' Chaim explained. "He needs the money most urgently."

"May I be so bold as to ask who this man is?" the man asked, full of curiosity.

"I cannot divulge his name," said R' Chaim. "But believe me, he is a man highly esteemed by all, a truly distinguished member of the community."

"I do not cast any doubts on your judgment, *Rebbe*," the rich man apologized, "but I would like to know why you are so concerned about him? I am prepared to give one thousand rubles for such a noble cause, aware that it will save you much trouble, but I insist on knowing to whom the money is going."

One thousand coins! A fortune! The eyes of R' Chaim's companion lit up at the thought of all that money. It would be a boon to the cause. Would it not be worthwhile for R' Chaim to divulge the recipient's name for the sake of this significant sum?

R' Chaim must have read his thoughts for he said emphatically, "All I can say is that this man always gave eagerly and generously to charitable causes. But, now, fortune has turned against him and he needs money himself. More than that I will not reveal."

The rabbi's flat reply aroused the rich man's curiosity all the more. He said, "I see that this man must be one of the pillars of the community. I am ready to help out with half the sum you have set out to raise in order to extricate him from his difficult situation. But I demand to know for whom I am giving the money."

His words fell on unwilling ears. R' Chaim was willing to forego that enormous sum rather than provide the name of the desperate man.

The man who accompanied him tried to convince the rabbi to agree to that simple condition, for the sum proposed would not come easily. "He promises not to reveal the name to a single soul," he reminded R' Chaim.

R' Chaim was firm. "I can truly appreciate the tremendous sum which is at stake," he replied, "but the honor of that prominent man who has fallen on hard times is many times more precious to me. I prefer to go from house to house and beg for paltry sums in order to obtain the required amount rather than disclose his name."

R' Chaim uttered these words with all the heat and determination of his forceful personality. They made a deep impression upon the rich man. He bent his head thoughtfully, then begged R' Chaim to step aside with him and enter his study for some words in private.

As soon as the door was shut behind them, the host burst into tears. His entire body was racked with sobs. *"Rebbe,"* he managed to say between gasps, "I, too, have had severe financial setbacks, but I was ashamed to tell anyone about my situation. I could not bear the thought of people talking about me behind my back and pitying me . . .

"But now," he continued, his voice quavering, "that you have come to my house on behalf of another such anonymous Jew who is in a similar situation, I decided that the time had come to unburden myself and tell you my troubles. It was not idle curiosity that prompted me to attempt to squeeze the man's name from you, *Rebbe.* I wanted to see how far I could trust you in keeping my secret.

"Please forgive me for having been so disrespectful as to put you to such a test," he wept. "But now that I see how trustworthy you are and how highly you regard a person's privacy, I have come to the conclusion that I, too, must tell you of my plight, at least for the sake of my starving family. I beg of you, help me out of this situation. Find some way to get me back on my feet. I dread the thought of being reduced to begging — which is, truly, what might happen."

R' Chaim heard the man's moving words and was deeply affected. He did not breathe a word of what he had heard, but a few days later, he was again knocking on the doors of the good people of the city, asking them for their assistance — this time for the second Jew, whose name he certainly did not divulge.

Thanks to R' Chaim's efforts, the man succeeded in overcoming his difficulties and within a short time, had returned to his former status. After the *tzaddik* passed away, the rich man revealed the story which R' Chaim had hidden deep in his heart and taken to the grave.

On this day, in 5574 (1814), R' David of Lelov passed away. He was born in 5506 (1746). R' David, the first of the Lelov dynasty, was known as a saintly man.

Doctor and Wonder-Worker

*D*r. Bernard was a famous Polish specialist. He was a member of a totally assimilated family who had no ties with the religious community. Nevertheless, the Jews of his city all consulted him in their need.

A wealthy Jew fell critically ill. Dr. Bernard was consulted. He examined the patient thoroughly and prescribed treatment.

But the rich man did not respond and again, Dr. Bernard was called in. He looked very grave. Turning to the family, he said somberly, "I am afraid that there is no hope."

With these words, he left the house, leaving a stunned family open mouthed and helpless.

"We must go to Lelov, to the *Rebbe!*" someone, suddenly, exclaimed. This call for action roused the entire family from its paralysis. The sons went to prepare the coach and soon were off to Lelov.

They were admitted into the *Rebbe's* presence at once. "*Rabbenu*," they said, "our father is on his deathbed. The doctor has already given up hope. Please pray for him and rouse Heavenly mercy."

They stood around, trembling with awe and fear, waiting for the *Rebbe's* verdict. R' David went over to a cupboard in the corner, took out a bottle of wine and some honey cake and handed them to the sons. "Hurry home and give the sick man some of this cake and wine. In the merit of the blessings he recites over them he will be granted a speedy recovery."

The sons thanked him and rushed homeward. They poured a cup of wine for their father and cut a slice of cake. The suffering man said the blessings, ate and drank. And lo! Only a short while later, he was already feeling better.

A few days passed, and from day to day his health improved until, finally, he was up and about, altogether cured.

His amazing recovery was the talk of the town. And since people all knew how it came about, they could not help marveling at R' David's miracle. "Look at that!" they said, "R' David succeeded in healing a case which even the great specialist had regarded as hopeless."

The report was so widespread that it even reached Dr. Bernard. He passed it off as a false rumor. But as he was walking down the street one day, he met that very patient whom he had thought to be long dead.

The doctor stopped in his tracks and looked at the man with wide-eyed amazement. He begged his erstwhile patient to tell him how he had recovered.

"A short while after you had given up on me, I ate some cake and drank some wine sent by R' David of Lelov. That was the turning point of my illness. I recovered soon afterwards."

Dr. Bernard could not forget the man's words even after he returned home. "From the medical standpoint," he reasoned to

R' Chaim David Bernard

himself, "eating cake and drinking wine could only have hastened the man's death. If he recovered, it can only be because of a miracle. It can only be due to the great merit of that saint, R' David of Lelov, who gave him the cake and wine."

Dr. Bernard was a changed man after that. Previously, he had been far removed from all religious practice; now he became a frequent visitor to R' David and, with the *Rebbe's* influence and guidance, repented and became a fervent *chasid.*

Dr. Bernard did not leave his practice; he continued to treat people and succeeded in saving many lives. People went so far as to say that when he went to visit his patients he was accompanied by the angel Refael himself!

It was not long before people began bringing the doctor *kvitlach* and gifts of money such as *chasidim* to a *Rebbe.* Dr. Bernard became renowned in the entire land as the great *tzaddik,* R' Chaim David Bernard.

This is the eighth day after Moshe *Rabbenu* had begun reviewing the Torah and explaining it to the Jewish people before his death.

Love for Torah

Upon returning from his son's wedding, which took place in Poland, R' Akiva Eiger stopped over for the night in a small village. He went to the local inn and, since he did not have his things with him, asked the innkeeper for a *sefer* from which he could study.

The innkeeper said, "My son, who studies in the city, has all my *sefarim*. The only one I have here is *Chiddushei HaRashba*."

R' Akiva Eiger took it, leafed through it and noticed that one page was missing. "Don't worry," he said to the innkeeper, "to repay your kindness, I will supply that page." And R' Akiva Eiger began writing the missing page, word for word, from memory. He then studied from the *sefer* for the remainder of the night.

By morning, everyone in the village knew that the leader of the generation was gracing them with his presence. All the prominent men and scholars came to pay their respects. But when they reached the inn they learned that R' Akiva Eiger had already left.

R' Shimon Sofer

The innkeeper showed them the page which he had added to the *Rashba*. The scholars fetched an undamaged copy and turned to the corresponding page. The two pages were identical, down to the last letter!

R' Shimon Sofer, who told the story, would add, "It is not my intention to tell this anecdote just to have people marvel at my grandfather's phenomenal memory. What is more remarkable is his great love for Torah and his burning desire to study. We see that the very words of the *Rashba* were deeply etched in his memory and on the tip of his tongue. Yet he spent the night studying them from the text as if that work had just been freshly transmitted from Sinai!

"Whoever toils in Torah with such fervor is assured that he will never forget it. And that is what one should envy!"

This is the ninth day after Moshe *Rabbenu* had begun reviewing and explaining the Torah prior to his death. Since then, the Torah has been studied, reviewed and explained in Houses of Study, and its scholars have been supported by our people.

"To Think Thoughts"

R' Chaim of Volozhin had a special messenger making the rounds of the wealthy householders in order to raise money for his *yeshivah*. This *shaliach* was under special orders from R' Chaim to be frugal in his personal expenses so that the bulk of the money would go to the upkeep of the *yeshivah*. In the early days of the *yeshivah*, the monies which he collected were sufficient to keep the institution running smoothly.

But with time the *yeshivah* grew and so did its expenses. But the income — the money which the *shaliach* raised — remained static.

Realizing the need for greater funds, the *shaliach* came to R' Chaim. "Most of my benefactors," he said, "look upon me as a common beggar and give me mere pennies. But if I wore expensive clothing and traveled in a fine coach of my own, I am sure that they would respect me and give larger contributions."

R' Chaim agreed to give him an allowance for expensive

clothing and a coach. And, indeed, with his changed image the *shaliach* had greater success. He would return from his trips with a full purse.

One of the *yeshivah*'s steady supporters was a certain villager who appreciated Torah and Torah scholars; he always gave a sizable sum for Volozhin. But, now, when the *shaliach* came by private coach in his new attire, the man refused to give a penny. "I am sorry, I have nothing for you this time," he said curtly.

"But, why?" asked the *shaliach*. "The *yeshivah* is bigger than ever and its expenses are ever greater. We need your help more than in the past!"

The villager was adamant. "I am not interested in supporting that institution any longer. That is final!"

The *shaliach* left the village and returned to Volozhin. When he reported to R' Chaim about the success of his trip, he could not help mentioning the villager's strange refusal to give charity. "I could always count on him for a generous donation," the man confessed, puzzled, "but now he declined to give a penny."

R' Chaim was similarly puzzled. "He must have a definite reason for his refusal," he said. "I will go to him myself and learn what has made him change his attitude."

R' Chaim soon reached the village. When the villager saw the illustrious *rosh yeshivah* standing on his very threshold, he became flustered. Bowing low, he ushered him into his home and lavished much attention upon him.

R' Chaim opened up the conversation with pleasantries, but soon got to the point. "What has happened this year? We have always been able to count on you; why did you suddenly stop contributing to our *yeshivah*?"

"I will tell you the truth," the villager said sadly. "Each year I gave gladly to help support such a worthy establishment as the Volozhin Yeshivah, and was proud to do so. I was convinced that every penny I gave went directly to the upkeep of the students who studied Torah day and night. But this year, when I saw the *shaliach* in his stylish suit, when I saw his splendid coach and horses, I understood that he was indulging in these luxuries from my money and the money of other worthy donors. This angered me and I decided to stop giving altogether!"

R' Chaim listened intently, thought for a moment and then replied, "You must surely remember that in *parashas Ki Sissa* we are taught that *Hashem* designated Betzalel to oversee the work of the *Mishkan*. *Hashem* filled him with 'the spirit of G-d in knowledge and intelligence and wisdom and in all work, to think thoughts to work with gold, silver and copper.'

"The question arises: What thoughts are involved in the craftsmanship of the metals? An artisan should be skilled in his field, but what does this have to do with thinking thoughts?

"But there is a deep meaning behind those simple words. For there were ascending degrees of sanctity with regard to the areas of the *Mishkan* itself — the courtyard, the Sanctuary and the Holy of Holies; and with regard to the vessels — the Ark, for example, was holier than lesser vessels. The same held true for the donations given for building and equipping the *Mishkan*. Some donors were poor, but gave their gold jewelry with all their hearts, with genuine fervor, for the sake of the *Mishkan*. Some rich people begrudged their gold and gave silver instead, while even stingier people, who loved their money more than they did the commandments, gave copper to fulfill their obligation.

"All of these donations were gathered to one central place from which Betzalel was to select his materials for the Courtyard, the Sanctuary and the Holy of Holies, for the Table, the Ark and the vessels of lesser holiness. But this posed a great problem. How was he to know whose gift to use for the most lofty of vessels and whose to use for the least important vessels? How could Betzalel differentiate between the materials brought wholeheartedly and those given begrudgingly?

"For this reason, Betzalel had to be able to 'think thoughts'. He had to descend to the depths of the intentions of each of the donors, to be able to differentiate the varying degrees of sanctity with which they had given their contributions. The gold which the poor man had brought at great sacrifice, but with all his heart, went for the building of the Holy of Holies. The rich man's silver went for lesser articles while the copper, which was given for appearances' sake, would go to the least important utensils.

"Which brings us to the matter at hand," R' Chaim explained. "The very same principle applies to the needs of a *yeshivah*. There are common expenses, as there are holy expenses. The students themselves and their needs are on the level of the Holy of Holies. Our representative, who travels about collecting money, is vested with a certain amount of holiness, while his horse and coach have a much lesser degree of importance and sanctity, even though they are also necessary, for they enable him to travel quickly and accomplish more.

"The same can be said for the donors themselves. There are some who give with all their hearts for the sake of Torah. Such money is used directly for the most sanctified needs of the *yeshivah*, for the upkeep of the students themselves. Others give hesitantly, begrudgingly. Their money, most probably, goes for the upkeep of the *shaliach*, while the third type of donor, the one who stints, his money is used for the expenses of horse and carriage.

"You are a person who always gave generously and willingly, with your whole heart. You can be sure that your donation reached the highest level and went directly for the student who toiled over his study."

R' Chaim's penetrating words found their way to the heart of the recalcitrant villager. He hastened to open his purse and give the *rosh yeshivah* his donation — twice that which it had always been before!

On this day, in 5542 (1782), R' Shalom Sharaabi passed away in Jerusalem. Born in Yemen in 5480 (1720), he was one of the pillars of Kabbalah among our people. He wrote prolifically on that subject. On his *yahrzeit,* thousands throng to pray at his grave on the Mount of Olives in Jerusalem.

Who Wrote the Notes?

*T*hroughout his childhood years in Yemen, R' Shalom Sharaabi yearned to go up to *Eretz Yisrael.* Later, this dream was realized and he chose Jerusalem as his dwelling place.

There was a *yeshivah* of Kabbalists in Jerusalem, at that time, known as Beit El. It was headed by the famous R' Gedalyah Chayun. It was R' Shalom's deepest wish to be accepted into this *yeshivah*, which only the greatest and holiest attended. R' Shalom went to R' Gedalyah and offered his services as *shammash*, caretaker.

The serious young man found favor in R' Gedalyah's eyes and he agreed to hire him.

R' Shalom fulfilled his duties with devotion and dedication. Every night he would wake up each of the scholars from their slumber and lead the way to the *beis midrash* with his lantern. When they began their studies, he would prepare a warm drink for them. R' Shalom joined them at midnight when they sat on the ground and mourned for the *Beis Hamikdash*.

During the day, when R' Gedalyah was giving a lecture or leading a discussion on some complex subject, the *shammash* would sit in a corner of the room reciting *Tehillim* or seemingly dozing off. The students did not doubt that their caretaker was a devout Jew, but they considered him simple and unlearned, certainly not fluent in Kabbalah.

They did not dream, even in their wildest dreams, that the meek *shammash* was actually following all of the lessons being taught and absorbing every word! Or that his knowledge in the revealed and the mystic was prodigious!

How were they to know such a thing? How were they to realize that while R' Gedalyah was grappling with a complex matter, their simple *shammash* already knew the answer to his question and was bursting to reveal it? R' Shalom knew the answers to all the difficult problems and he would think to himself, "If only I dared tell R' Gedalyah what I know, his eyes would light up!"

But as vast as was his wisdom, so much greater was his humility. He kept the answers to himself, preferring to remain unknown.

R' Shalom kept his silence, but his heart was not at rest. He was troubled that R' Gedalyah and all the other scholars were toiling over the problems for which he had the answer! "Is it better," he asked himself, "to become recognized as a scholar by revealing the answers or to keep quiet and see them suffer?"

He struggled with his dilemma until he found the perfect solution: "I will write the answer on a piece of paper and after

the lesson, when all have gone home, I will place it between the pages of R' Gedalyah's *sefer*."

And so, one day, he did. No one was present to notice the *shammash* inserting his note inside the *rosh yeshivah's* copy.

R' Gedalyah was plagued by the difficult question and could find no rest. He could not eat, or even take a nap. He paced the floor, racking his brain. He sought the answer in books and manuscripts, but all in vain.

Small wonder, then, that by the time he returned to the *beis midrash* he was restless and despondent. He entered the room, bowed, only to meet the same gloomy expressions reflected upon the other scholars. They, too, had sought an answer to the difficult question, but had similarly failed. They had hoped to hear the answer from their master ...

R' Gedalyah went to his place and opened up his *sefer* at the designated place when he saw the note. He lifted it up and read it; his face paled with excitement and wonder. In a few measured words the difficult question had been clarified and answered!

His joyful expression did not escape the other scholars. But before they had a chance to ask, R' Gedalyah read the contents of the note — the solution to their problem.

"The writer of these lines is requested to step up front," the *rosh yeshivah* said, after reading the note aloud.

No one moved. R' Shalom, sitting in his remote corner, knew that these words were not directed at him, for R' Gedalyah surely did not suspect him of having written it. How happy he was, having caused that smile to light up R' Gedalyah's face without having had to reveal himself.

And from that day on, whenever the scholars at Beit El had a difficult problem which they could not solve themselves, they always found the answer in a note inserted inside the *rosh yeshivah's sefer*.

R' Gedalyah marveled and spoke about the matter at home.

Chanah, his daughter, decided to keep her eyes open and see what she could learn. When all of the scholars left the *beis midrash*, she secretly watched the young *shammash* and saw him take up her father's *sefer*, turn the pages and then return it to the table.

That evening she reported to her father, "I saw the *shammash* leafing through your *sefer*, Father. Perhaps he is the one behind the mysterious notes. Perhaps he is one of the thirty-six hidden *tzaddikim*."

The idea was strange, but he sent for the *shammash*, nevertheless. "In my capacity as rabbi," he said to the confused Shalom, "I order you to admit the truth: Are you the writer of all these notes?"

R' Shalom turned ashen. How had his secret been revealed? And what should he do now? He certainly could not defy the *rosh yeshivah*'s order by hiding the truth. He could not lie. And so, he said as softly as he could, "Yes, I wrote the answers on those notes. *Hashem* blessed me with understanding to reach the solutions to the problems." His voice broke and he pleaded, "I beg of you, don't tell anyone of your discovery."

R' Gedalyah rose from his seat and embraced the young man heartily. "R' Shalom! If *Hashem* has indeed blessed you with such amazing intelligence, then you must be wise beyond compare. You deserve to be *rosh yeshivah* in my place! If you have acquired so much knowledge, it is sinful to keep it all to yourself! The time has come for you to reveal yourself to the world."

His secret was out and on that very day the scholars of Beit El appointed R' Shalom Sharaabi as their *rosh yeshivah*.

On this day, in 5598 (1838), the Chafetz Chaim was born. He died on the 24th of *Elul* 5693 (1933). The Chafetz Chaim was one of the most famous leaders our people have known.

Don't Damage the Railroad Tracks

*T*hroughout his life R' Yisrael Meir Hakohen of Radin, the Chafetz Chaim, was known as an assiduous scholar, the perfect example of the verse, "And you shall think on it day and night."

He was a young man when he came to live in Radin, which is south of Vilna. He opened up a small grocery to support himself but every free moment he returned to his *sefarim*.

Time passed and the Chafetz Chaim founded a *yeshivah* in Radin. Its fame spread throughout Europe and students from near and far thronged to Radin to acquire a Torah education there.

From the time of its establishment, the Chafetz Chaim devoted all of his time only to the study of Torah and its dissemination.

The study of Torah was so dear and vital to him that when he recited the *vidui* (confession of sins) which one says during the morning prayers after the *shemoneh esrei*, he would add

The Chafetz Chaim

to the sins of the letter *beis: "batalnu min haTorah* — we have wasted time from study."

When a *gaon* such as the Chafetz Chaim would utter these words in a trembling voice, people would gaze in wonder. How could this saintly man, whose days and nights were totally devoted to Torah, suspect that he had been lax in that very aspect?

Once, when the Chafetz Chaim entered the *beis medrash* of the Yeshivah of Radin, he saw a large group of students conversing instead of learning.

He strode determinedly towards them, without their noticing him, and when he reached the group, he said, "Since you are already wasting time from your studies, let me tell you a story which I heard from R' Yisrael of Salant, founder of the *musar* movement."

The abashed students stood there, silent, listening to the tale.

"A man once lost his senses," the Chafetz Chaim began, "and without reason began dismantling the nearby railroad tracks. Some passersby noticed it and shouted at him, 'Why are you damaging the railroad? Don't you realize that you are endangering the lives of many train passengers?' The man looked up blankly and replied, 'Why? The railroad stretches for hundreds, even thousands of miles on either side. What difference does it make if I damage only a few yards?'

"This story has a moral," the Chafetz Chaim continued, in an excited voice. "If a Jew stops studying Torah for even a short interval and says that it doesn't matter because Torah has been studied continuously since it was given at Sinai, and, anyway, at this very moment there are many scholars engrossed in study, he is like that demented man who ripped up only a few yards of an immensely long railroad and refused to see that he was endangering hundreds of lives.

"The hazard is the very same, if even only a few of us cease our study for a short while. We are endangering all of the future generations!"

The young men accepted the rebuke and returned, one by one, to their places. Within moments, the large hall resounded with the reassuring sound of Torah being studied by all.

Fulfilling One's Duty

The communal leaders of Bialystock, Russia were gathered to discuss strengthening the worthy institution of *Vaad Hayeshivos*. The Chafetz Chaim, founder of that body, also attended. Upon the conclusion of the session, he invited all of the wealthy men of the city to his inn and said, "I expect each one of you to pledge a specific amount for the *Vaad Hayeshivos*."

All of those present agreed — except for one. He stubbornly refused to commit himself for the amount requested of him. "Look at this," he said to the others, waving a fat sheaf of receipts. "I have already given huge amounts to support *yeshivos* and I think that I have already fulfilled my duty in supporting Torah."

When the Chafetz Chaim heard his remark, he turned to the man and said, "I hear that you think you have already fulfilled your obligation towards the support of Torah. One can do one's duty and 'get by' in various ways. When it comes to eating, for example, some can subsist on dry bread and a morsel of potatoes in a watery soup throughout their lives and be perfectly satisfied. As for housing, many large families make do with cramped quarters and still manage. When it comes to clothing, peasants wear coarse materials and clumsy shoes, but consider themselves protected from the elements. All these people get by with the minimum. But you would not be satisfied with such a standard. You eat heartily each day of the best of foods, live in spacious housing furnished with the latest modern comforts and wear expensive clothing.

"You may say that people should be free to live according

to the means with which they are blessed. If *Hashem* saw fit to grant them the resources to eat and live well, why shouldn't they make use of them? Why must one just 'get by' if he can live well and enjoy the bounty which is his?

"If that is your argument, if you think that your wealth is yours to enjoy, to make life easier and more pleasant for you, not simply to 'manage' or 'get by', then know that you must fulfill your obligation of charity and support of Torah in that same measure — generously, in accordance with your high standard of living.

"After you have filled your hundred and twenty years and you appear before the Heavenly Court in the World of Truth, you will be asked, 'Did you give charity? Did you donate to *yeshivos*? Did you support Torah scholars?' Will you also wave your bundle of receipts and say, 'Look! I gave all this away!' Will you acquit yourself with that alone?

"They will look at you and say, 'Fine. Admirable. You have fulfilled your obligation,' and they will admit you to Gan Eden. There you will see Torah scholars seated at golden tables together with the philanthropists who gave generously to support Torah, beyond their minimal obligations.

"And you? You will stand by the sidelines. No one will pay any attention to you. You will not even be invited to sit at a table. And you will wonder why. Had you not, also, supported *yeshivos* and Torah scholars? And as proof, you will again flutter the receipts in your hand.

"And what will they reply to you then? They will ask you why you are angry and resentful. You only gave to fulfill your minimum obligation. Here, then, is your minimal reward, measure for measure. We also discharge our obligations . . ."

This was the twelfth of the forty days during which Moshe *Rabbenu* reviewed and explained the Torah to Israel before he departed from this world.

It Is no Mitzvah to Be a Scholar

One of the followers of R' Mendel of Kotzk came to pour out his troubled heart before the *Rebbe*. He said, "I have a poor memory, which greatly hinders me in my study of Torah. No matter how much I strive and yearn to study and become a great scholar, I am held back by my weak memory. What can I do? My memory fails me. Whenever I learn something, I promptly forget it."

"Who told you that you must become a learned man?" asked the *Rebbe*. "Is it not sufficient for you to be a decent, upright Jew who studies Torah because he was thus commanded?"

And with that, R' Mendel went over to the bookcase and took out a *Tanach*. He held it up before the confused *chasid* and said, "Nowhere in the entire Torah does it state that a person must strive to be a great scholar!" He leafed through the *sefer* until he reached the first chapter in *Yeshayahu*. "Here," he said, pointing, "even the prophet says, 'Study diligently,' upon which Rashi comments, 'We learn from here that the purpose of study is not for a person to become erudite and learned but in order for him to become a better man, one who always does good'."

On this day in 5570 (1810), R' Mordechai of Lechovitz passed away. A saintly man, he was the founder of several chasidic dynasties including that of Kobrin and Slonim.

Together in Life and Death

Even though they lived a great distance from one another, R' Mordechai of Lechovitz and R' Avraham of Kalisk enjoyed a strong mutual affection.

On the fourth of *Shevat*, a week before R' Mordechai's death, R' Avraham of Kalisk passed away in Teveryah. And on that day the *menorah* in R' Mordechai's house fell and its lights were extinguished. R' Mordechai intoned, "R' Avraham has just died in Teveryah."

Only a few hours later he received a letter from R' Avraham which had been written several days before his death. It hinted that he was about to die and that his good friend, R' Mordechai, would follow him to the grave shortly.

And so it was. On the thirteenth of *Shevat*, R' Mordechai's soul also rose up to the vaults of Heaven.

An Opportune Moment

The wedding meal of one of the family of R' Mordechai of Lechovitz was over. The *tzaddik* arose and was about to leave the room when one of his *chasidim* detained him.

"Ah, Reb Nachum," said the *Rebbe*, "what is it?"

Reb Nachum replied, "I once heard the *Rebbe* say that when a wedding is celebrated in the royal family it is a time of favor, an opportune moment. I, therefore, have a request to make of the king, the *Rebbe*, that is."

"What is your wish? It shall be granted!" R' Mordechai declared.

"I want to be rid of the bad habit of anger," said Reb Nachum.

The *Rebbe* promised to fulfill this request. And indeed, from that time until his death Reb Nachum never became angry. Not even once!

Thanks for the Beard

A simple Jew once came to R' Mordechai of Lechovitz. Although he was a mere tailor, as soon as the *Rebbe* beheld him, he rose and stood before him.

Those present marveled. Why had the Rebbe risen for a common tailor?

Later, when he left, R' Mordechai turned to the others and said, "I saw the tailor's beard radiating a great light."

The *tzaddik*'s words aroused the *chasidim*'s curiosity and they ran out after the tailor. They soon overtook him and in the course of their conversation, the tailor said, "Each day when I rise I think to myself: What purpose do I fulfill in this world? And I am filled with sadness and pain for I am not a person of many worthy deeds. But then I remind myself of one commandment that I do observe, of not cutting one's beard, and that fills me with joy. I thank *Hashem* for my beard and for the *mitzvah* which it fulfills."

When the *chasidim* heard the simple tailor's words, they were no longer surprised at the deference shown to him by the Rebbe.

14 Shevat

On the evening of this day, that is, the eve of the fifteenth of *Shevat*, in 5645 (1885), R' Ezra Atiyah was born in Syria. He later went up to Jerusalem and was appointed as the *rosh yeshivah* of Porat Yosef. Aside from his greatness in Torah, he was also known as an exemplary *tzaddik*. R' Ezra Atiyah passed away on the nineteenth of *Iyar*, 5730 (1970).

The Unpaid Assistant

During the period that R' Ezra Atiyah stood at its head, Yeshivat Porat Yosef did not only have financial worries to contend with in those difficult times of poverty and want. It had an even more

R' Ezra Atiyah

trying challenge — the bitter struggle against the parents of its students. Due to the strangling poverty of those times in Jerusalem, many parents took their children out of *yeshivos* to send them to work. And so the unfortunate boys pulled in one direction — they wished to study more and more — while their parents tugged in a different direction — they wanted their sons to learn a trade.

It thus happened that a father of one of the more gifted students once visited the *yeshivah*. The son was deeply engrossed in the study of a complex problem in the *gemara* when his father rushed up to him, seized him by the arm and began dragging him along. "You are coming with me to the shop," he said. "You are needed there far more than here."

Miserable and disappointed, the son let himself be pulled along, though he looked back longingly at the table with the *gemara* lying upon it. But what could he do — this was his father. He owed him obedience and respect.

When they reached the entrance of the *beis midrash* they were confronted by R' Ezra Atiyah. The father squirmed uncomfortably and began justifying himself, "If my son does not come now to help me, I will have to hire an assistant. But I cannot afford extra help at the moment."

"Do you know what?" R' Ezra suggested, removing his coat and rolling up his sleeves. "Let the boy remain here. I will come with you and help in the store. At no charge!"

The father was dumb struck. He left the *yeshivah* without uttering another word, leaving both his son and R' Ezra, the unpaid assistant, behind.

That very lad, whom the business world had to forego, became one of the luminaries of the Torah world ...

Permission to Rule

R' Ezra Atiyah bore a deep love and respect for all those who studied and valued Torah — all, that is, except for one: himself. When young rabbis came to visit, he would stand to his full height and treat them as if they were venerable scholars and not even feel that he was greater than they.

It is told that when he once visited Cairo he was asked a difficult question by a local resident. R' Ezra puzzled over the matter at length and finally arrived at a *p'sak* (ruling). But, before giving the decision, he said, "I must first ask permission of the rabbi of the city before giving my *p'sak*."

The man who had asked the question was surprised, but he agreed to accompany the visiting *rosh yeshivah* to the rabbi of Cairo.

It was a long distance to his home and the weather unbearably hot, but R' Ezra was undaunted. When he arrived, he presented the question. He quoted *rishonim* and *acharonim* and brought proofs from all over the *gemara* and *poskim* to uphold his opinion. When he was finished, he waited for the rabbi's decision. The rabbi said, "If everything is so clear, why have you come to me?"

"I wanted the rabbi's permission to rule on the question, since you are the authority here," he said simply.

Who Made Room for Whom?

At a meeting of rabbis in which R' Ezra Atiyah participated, his eye fell upon a certain young rabbi who had arrived late and had no place to sit. R' Ezra beckoned to him and whispered, "I don't feel well. I am leaving. Here, take my seat."

When he left the auditorium, he turned to a companion, "Had I said to that young man that I wanted to give him a seat to honor him, he would surely have refused. That is why I added that I did not feel well."

"But he would have been justified in refusing to take the seat you vacated for him," the companion commented. "Why should you get up for a young man?"

"Why not?" R' Ezra retorted. "He may be younger than I, but he is nonetheless a scholar!"

This day is the *Rosh Hashanah* of trees. On this day it is a custom to eat fruits of the seven species, *shivas haminim*, which flourish in *Eretz Yisrael*.

A Bitter Pomegranate with a Sweet Ending

*T*he entire town was speaking of nothing else. It was on everyone's mind, on everyone's lips. The Eisen family, one of Poland's most prominent, was about to leave for *Eretz Yisrael*.

When the townspeople learned of this, they had mixed feelings. They were happy that the Eisens had the good fortune of fulfilling every Jew's desire. Nevertheless, they had been a distinguished part of the community for many generations, esteemed and beloved by all. Parting with them was most difficult. To tell the truth, some people even envied them the privilege and secretly asked themselves why they were not doing that very same thing.

The town simmered with the news while the Eisen home seethed with activity. Aside from the frenzied preparations for such a long journey, the members of the family had to prepare themselves emotionally, as well. One thread ran through all of their thoughts: What must they do to make themselves worthy of treading upon holy soil? How could they prepare themselves for the privilege of being numbered among the inhabitants of Jerusalem?

The awaited day arrived. The Eisens said their good-byes with mixed feelings of sadness and expectation. The entire community turned out to see them off. "Please," was their final request, "pray for us at the holy sites in *Eretz Yisrael*."

After a long, arduous journey, the Eisens found themselves at the port, about to board ship for the Holy Land. In those times, a sea voyage was no pleasure cruise. The ships were hardly seaworthy and the journey among rough seas sometimes took many weeks or months. But the Eisens paid no attention to that. All their hardships were inconsequential in face of their goal — to reach *Eretz Yisrael*. This vision overcame all difficulties and made them forget all their suffering.

Finally, the long voyage came to an end and the ship docked on the shores of the Holy Land. The Eisens went down the gangplank timorously, awed by the idea of finally treading on sanctified soil. One by one, they bent down to kiss the earth. "Let us hope that we prove worthy to dwell upon this holy soil," they prayed tearfully.

After the initial excitement died down, they set out on the next lap of their journey to the city which they had chosen as their new home — Jerusalem.

The trip to Jerusalem took several days. They wended their way over mountain passages in horse-drawn wagons. But even this exhausting mode of travel did not faze the Eisens. Their hearts yearned for one thing only — to behold the Holy City.

Soon, the mountains of Judea loomed up before them, bathed in golden sunlight. The splendid spectacle of glory and grandeur made their hearts beat with excitement. And thus overcome with emotion, they completed their journey and reached the gates of Jerusalem.

And there, at the gates of the city, a surprise awaited them. A vendor stood by the roadside. "Pomegranates! Pome-

granates!" he cried. "Have some juicy red pomegranates!"

The new immigrants looked at the produce. What was he selling? They had never seen such fruit. They swarmed about him, filled with curiosity. The vendor held one up and explained, "This is the *rimon*, one of the seven species in which *Eretz Yisrael* abounds!"

"A *rimon . . . shivas haminim*," the members of the family echoed with feeling. They gave him some money without hesitation and let him weigh some of the beautiful, luscious-looking purple-red fruits.

They sat down near the wall and the head of the family cut a pomegranate and gave portions to the others.

How excited they were to recite the blessing and to savor the exotic fruit. But they were greatly disappointed, for the fruit which they tasted for the first time was bitter. The children pursed their lips and whispered to one another, "This is not at all tasty. It's bitter, not sweet."

The whispers and the sour looks on his family's face shocked the father. "How can you think anything evil about the fruits of the Holy Land?" he said sternly. Yet, he could not deny that they were telling the truth and this pained him all the more! He asked himself, "How have we sinned that we are not worthy of enjoying the good taste of the fruits of *Eretz Yisrael*?"

With an expression of acute pain, he continued, "We must not speak ill of the fruits of *Eretz Yisrael*, the very fruits which the Torah praises. It can only be our sins which have caused us to find fault with these blessed fruits and prevent us from enjoying them. The only thing to do, in that case, is to hasten to the *Kosel Hamaaravi* and to pray before the Almighty. We must repent of our sins and then, perhaps, we will be granted the privilege of enjoying the fruits of our Holy Land."

The family arose and began walking behind the father

towards the Western Wall. Their excitement mounted with each step and when they found themselves standing before the spot from which the *Shechinah* had never departed — they were beside themselves with emotion.

They stood there, the immigrant family from Poland, for a long time, pouring forth their tears and prayers by the *Kosel*. They begged *Hashem* to enable them to do *teshuvah*, to repent with all their hearts. Finally, with eyes still lingering longingly upon the Wall, they departed.

Only now did they turn to the city to find lodgings. They were accepted at the *hachnasas orchim* hostel where they ate and rested.

Towards *minchah*-time, the father went to one of the many synagogues which glorified Jerusalem. The regular worshipers noticed the newcomer at once and welcomed him warmly into their midst. They did everything they could to make him feel at home.

Jerusalemites of those times, all brilliant scholars, invariably turned the conversation to Torah subjects. And since they wished to include matters of the day, the talk revolved around the sanctity of the land, the city and the *Beis Hamikdash*.

"Do you know," the newcomer mentioned, "that when we reached Jerusalem we bought some pomegranates. It was the first time that I had seen this fruit. We were thrilled at the opportunity to taste it but," a note of pain crept into his voice, "we were disappointed. The pomegranate was not sweet at all, but bitter. It must be my sins and the sins of my family that prevented us from savoring the sweetness of the wonderful fruits of *Eretz Yisrael*."

"A bitter pomegranate?" the people wondered. "How can that be? Most pomegranates are sweet or at worst, tangy or pleasantly sour. But there is no such thing as a bitter pomegranate!"

There was a clever Jew among the group who had been listening to the conversation. He turned to the guest and asked, "Tell me, how did you eat the pomegranate?"

"What do you mean?" the Polish Jew asked in turn. "We ate it like you eat any fruit. We ate the meat of the fruit and discarded the seeds."

Smiles tugged at the corners of the mouths of all those listening. They now understood why he had found the pomegranate bitter. "Don't feel bad," they said. "It is not your sins that are to blame for your family finding the fruit bitter. You simply did not know how to eat it."

He looked at them bewildered, but the man next to him explained, "A pomegranate is different from other fruits. Instead of eating the flesh and casting away the seeds, you eat the seeds and throw away the peel."

One of the men rushed home and returned with a few pomegranates. He peeled one and offered it to the guest. Having already learned the rules of eating this fruit, the newcomer recited the benediction and sank his teeth into the juicy red seeds. His eyes lit up! It was as sweet as honey!

As the juice flowed down his throat, he felt as if a heavy stone were being lifted off his heart. So it was not the sins of his family which had prevented them from enjoying the fruit, only a simple mistake. That appealed to him even more than the actual experience of tasting the new fruit.

Happy and light hearted, he returned to his lodgings after the evening prayers. Seeing his face alight, his family understood that something wonderful had happened to their father.

He took out the pomegranate which he had received from the man in the synagogue and served it to his family. "You are supposed to eat the seeds and throw away the peel," he instructed them.

They said the blessing and bit into the seeds. A delectable

juice squirted down their throats. "What a marvelous fruit!" the children exclaimed joyfully to one another. This time they were not afraid to voice their opinions. "We have never tasted such a delicious fruit!" The adults also enjoyed eating more and more of the seeds.

And, just like their father, they rejoiced in the exotic fruit but were even more enthralled with the realization that they had not been deprived of the sweetness of the fruits of *Eretz Yisrael* because of their sins.

When the father saw his family so captivated by the experience, he rose to his feet and said, "My dear children, we have learned something very important today. When a person cannot perceive what is good and beautiful in the Land and its fruits, he must realize that it stems from a misjudgment. The Land is not to blame — he is the one at fault. For one thing is clear beyond doubt — *Eretz Yisrael* is good and its fruits superior!"

On this day, in 5671 (1911), R' Shalom Mordechai
Hakohen Shwadron, rabbi of Brezan, passed way. R'
Shalom Mordechai was born on the 27th of *Sivan*,
5595 (1835), and was one of the most prominent
poskim of the last generation. He wrote "Responsa
of the Maharsham".

Defendant in a Dream

One of the important influences upon R' Shalom
Mordechai Shwadron was his teacher, R'
Yitzchak Isaac of Zidichov. The teacher-*talmid*
relationship arose from a most unusual event which
R' Shalom Mordechai's son told as he had heard it from his
father:

R' Shalom Mordechai became ill with typhus, an often fatal
disease. He lay critically ill. When he was at death's door, he
had a dream. He stood before the Heavenly Court and was
sentenced to die. But at the last moment, someone came
running up to the bench. It was R' Yitzchak Isaac of Zidichov,
who wished to testify on behalf of the defendant. He spoke in
his favor and was able to commute the sentence.

From that moment on, R' Shalom Mordechai's health began
to improve. As soon as he was well, he traveled to Zidichov to
visit R' Yitzchak Isaac, whom he had never met before.

When he stood before the *tzaddik*, his heart began pound-

R' Shalom Mordechai Shwadron

ing. There sat the very figure who had appeared in his dream and defended him. From then on he became his devoted disciple and adherent.

A Friday Night Dream

His son tells of another interesting dream which R' Shalom Mordechai had:

One Friday night R' Shalom Mordechai dreamed that he was again standing before the Heavenly Court, attending the trial of a certain young man who was accused of having desecrated the *Shabbos*. The court ruled that he must die.

When he awoke the next morning, the *tzaddik* was in a quandary. "Should I tell the young man what I dreamed, or not?" he wondered. He finally decided that if the man in question approached him after prayers and wished him a '*Gut Shabbos*' and spoke to him 'in learning', he would reveal what he had seen.

The young man did approach R' Shalom Mordechai after prayers, but instead of conversing with the rabbi, he burst into tears. "*Rebbe*," he blurted, "something terrible happened to me yesterday. As I was sitting at the table and studying, my pipe in mouth, I became so engrossed that I did not even realize that *Shabbos* had already arrived and I continued to smoke!"

When the *tzaddik* heard this, he calmed the young man and told him to come to him after *Shabbos* and he would prescribe a form of *teshuvah*. The man's life was saved, thanks to R' Shalom Mordechai's dream and his good advice.

The First Sermon

It is told that during the last hours of his life, with his dying breath, R' Shalom Mordechai was offered some wine to strengthen him.

He refused, saying, "It is a stated *halachah* that whoever drinks wine is not permitted to give a ruling on Torah law. I must now prepare my first scholarly sermon before the Heavenly Academy and I must, therefore, abstain from drinking wine."

On this day, in 5615 (1855), R' Yechezkel of Kazimir passed away. He was a saintly person and one of the foremost personalities of the Chasidic movement.

Shavuos on Mount Sinai

*W*hen *chasidim* sought to crown R' Shlomo of Radomsk, author of *Tiferes Shlomo*, as their *Rebbe*, he turned them down.

Shavuos came. All week long *chasidim* had begun flocking to him from many towns and villages, desiring to spend the Festival with him. When R' Shlomo saw their numbers, he became angry and said, "Go away. I am not a *Rebbe* and I will not let you enter."

But the *chasidim* did not obey. On the morrow their numbers had increased!

R' Shlomo went to R' Yechezkel of Kazimir to spend the *Yom Tov* with him, leaving the throngs behind in Radomsk.

When he reached Kazimir, R' Yechezkel showed his surprise. After greeting him, he asked, "What are you doing here? How can you leave such a large flock of Jews without a shepherd and come here? Upon the verse, 'And Moshe descended from the mountain to the people', Rashi explains that 'this teaches us that Moshe did not return to his personal affairs but went from the mountain to the people and from the people to the mountain.' But what affairs could Moshe have had in the desert? What business did he have to tend to? The answer is that each Jew had made extensive preparations for the Festival of the Giving of the Torah, each man according to his stature. Moshe *Rabbenu*, who was the greatest and holiest of them all, required the greatest degree of preparation for this momentous event. And yet, he did not turn to his personal preparations. He did not think of *his* stature and *his* affairs, but was concerned about Israel as a whole. This is what Rashi means by the words 'from the mountain to the people and from the people to the mountain.' How, then," R' Yechezkel looked sternly at R' Shlomo and continued, "could you have left the people in Radomsk and run away to Kazimir?"

But the *Tiferes Shlomo* had an answer: "Moshe *Rabbenu* was at Mount Sinai, a place suffused with holiness. He did not require preparation. Like Moshe, I would also like to be by Mount Sinai . . . ," he said allegorically.

R' Yechezkel did not reply. And so, R' Shlomo remained to spend the Festival with his *Rebbe*.

That *Shavuos* was different from any other. The *chasidim* who were there were to later say that, whoever had not spent that *Shavuos* in Kazimir never tasted a real *Shavuos* in his life!

R' Yechezkel honored R' Shlomo with the saying of the *Akdamus*, since he was gifted with a rare musical talent. A choir of eighty *chasidim* accompanied him as his voice soared into majestic crescendos.

And then it seemed to all those present as if the walls and windows of the *beis knesses* reverberated with the mighty sound.

And the hearts of the listeners melted away from the sheer beauty and sweetness of that *Akdamus* in Kazimir.

This is the eighteenth day of the forty during which Moshe *Rabbenu* reviewed and explained the Torah before his death.

The Question — and the Answer

R' Yitzchak Elchanan Spector of Kovno had just received an express letter from a young Lithuanian rabbi. The long letter dealt with a difficult question which had arisen in the *gemara*. At the end, the rabbi wrote, "I am eagerly waiting for you to answer my question so that I can continue my studies with a peaceful mind."

This is the reply which the young rabbi received from the rabbi of Kovno: "Look up the *gemara* in *Menachos* on page so-and-so and the *Tosafos* there — and your mind will be at peace."

The rabbi turned quickly to the source indicated. He studied all of the remarks of *Tosafos*, but to his great perplexity, could find no connection between the question he had asked and the matter dealt with there!

Without hesitation, he sent another letter off to R' Yitzchak Elchanan and said, "Can there have been some mistake in the page number which you told me to look up?"

R' Yitzchak Elchanan Spector

A reply from the rabbi of Kovno was soon forthcoming. "My first letter was correct. If you examine the *Tosafos* there, you will find a question without an answer. And still, the authors of the *Tosafos* continued on with their labor in Torah, their minds at peace in spite of the unanswered question . . ."

On this day in 5696 (1936), R' Menachem Mendel Landau passed away. A famous Kabbalist, he was the first *Admor* of Strikov, a figure most esteemed and admired by all Polish *chasidim* and famed for his vast wisdom throughout the world of Torah.

At the Right Time

In the years directly preceding the Holocaust, R' Menachem Mendel Landau of Strikov became especially renowned as a policy maker for world Jewry. Jewish leaders and chasidic figures consulted with him, for he embodied all of the virtues which our Sages deemed necessary in a leader. He was well versed in all the revealed and the mystic areas of Torah, devout in all of his deeds, good and benevolent to all and yet fearless and unintimidated by anyone; a man of firm conviction.

And to crown all of his fine characteristics was his outstanding acts of charity to individual Jews. The poverty and hardships of his unfortunate brothers were his primary, daily concern, to such a degree, that Polish Jews would say that the Strikover *Rebbe* was to Poland what R' Chaim of Sanz had been to Galicia and Hungary. It is known that the *Divrei Chaim* of Sanz would not suffer a coin to remain in his house overnight, if it could help a suffering Jew.

He was also erudite in *halachah*, and observed it to the letter, especially the laws of charity. He knew how to give and when, to whom one gave first and to whom last. With the increased immigration to *Eretz Yisrael* during his days and the development of the settlement there, he labored diligently to raise funds for the impoverished residents who lacked the sources of minimal income, reminding people of the halachic requirement to "support the poor of *Eretz Yisrael* in preference to those abroad."

The *Rebbe* of Strikov visited the Holy Land twice and traversed its entire length and breadth, first in 5684 (1924) and again, before his death in 5695 (1935). During his stay he devoted himself to improve the conditions of its inhabitants, principally the poor of Jerusalem, who were to remember him gratefully for many years to come.

One elder of Jerusalem tells of his visit in 5684 (1924). At that time, there was a relative newcomer to Jerusalem, considered well-to-do by those standards, but somewhat tightfisted. The *Admor* of Strikov arrived during the very week that he was celebrating his son's *bar-mitzvah*.

"What a great honor it would be if the celebrated *tzaddik* would grace my celebration with his presence," he thought to himself. 'I will go myself and invite him to my *simchah*."

He went to the *Rebbe's* lodgings in the Bucharin quarter. The *Rebbe* accepted his invitation but upon one condition:

"I agree to participate in your *simchah*, but it will cost you a great deal. I demand twenty-five pounds," the elderly *Admor* announced. That was an enormous sum for those times.

The Jerusalemite had no choice but to agree. He began counting out the money.

In the midst of the transaction, the *Rebbe* called his son (and successor), R' Yaakov Yitzchak Dan, and asked him to

R' Menachem Mendel Landau with his son R' Yaakov Yitzchak Dan

deliver the entire sum to a certain address in the Beis Yisrael section.

Who lived there? And why had the *Rebbe* of Strikov humbled himself before the Jerusalemite and made his attendance dependent on a fee?

That house was the home of a large family. Their oldest daughter was to be married in a month, but the family, which never even had enough money for their *Shabbos* expenses, had been unable to fulfill their promises of a dowry and the *chasan's* side refused to set a date for the wedding.

And then the *Rebbe's* son appeared. R' Yaakov Yitzchak Dan laid the twenty-five pounds on the table — the very amount that was required for the dowry. Joy flowed over in that home.

As he had promised, the *Rebbe* of Strikov attended the *bar-mitzvah* celebration together with his son and his entourage.

While still in Jerusalem, the *Admor* was able to attend the wedding and, as it turned out, the funeral of that Jerusalemite who had made it possible, as well.

It was not for naught that the population of Jerusalem fondly remembered this great man. And when he returned in 5696 (1936), old and feeble, they flocked to bask in his light and to receive his holy blessing. The cream of Jerusalem scholars were privileged to sit at his 'table' and benefit from his exalted presence.

On this day in 2320 (1440 B.C.E.), Asher ben Yaakov *Avinu* was born.

"I Shall Indeed Remember"

Our Sages said that Yaakov *Avinu* was prophetically told that his sons would be redeemed from Egypt by a messenger of *Hashem*, a man who would address them with the phrase *"pakod pakadeti* — I shall indeed remember."

Yaakov *Avinu* transmitted this secret to his son, Yosef, and Yosef told it to his brother, Asher. Asher disclosed it to his daughter, Serach, for he knew that she would still be alive at the time of the Exodus:

And then Asher told his daughter, "The true redeemer is one who comes and uses the expression *'pakod pakadeti'."*

When the time came, Moshe *Rabbenu* came as a Heavenly emissary to redeem the Jews. But the Jews were doubtful and hesitant. Was he a real savior?

The Elders went to Serach bas Asher for advice. She asked them, "What words did this messenger use?"

They replied, *"Pakod pakadeti."*

"If so, then he is genuine."

The people put their faith in Moshe and believed the news of the imminent redemption which he foretold.

She Rejoiced and Was Rewarded

Serach, the daughter of Asher, was blessed with a very long life.

Our Sages tell us in the *Midrash*:

When the brothers of Yosef learned that he was still alive and the ruler over all of Egypt, they hastened back to Yaakov, their father, in Canaan, to tell him the good news.

They knew, however, that if Yaakov heard the tidings without being prepared, he might die of shock. They, therefore, took counsel and discussed the best way to break the news gently.

They pondered the problem all along the way. When they approached their home, they beheld Serach coming towards them. Serach was a clever girl and also musically talented. As soon as they saw her, the brothers knew instinctively what to do!

They told her to fetch her harp. "Go to your grandfather, Yaakov *Avinu*, and play some music for him. And sing a soft accompaniment: 'My uncle Yosef is alive and he is the ruler over all of Egypt'."

Instrument in hand, Serach hurried to her grandfather's house and did as her uncles had said. She played soothingly and sang her sweet message. Yaakov listened and was enthralled. And then joy entered his heart and the spirit of *Hashem* rested upon him.

As a reward for her fine deed, Yaakov blessed Serach, saying, "Since you gladdened my spirit, you shall be rewarded with long life. You will never die."

Yaakov's blessing was realized. Serach bas Asher lived a full, long life and was privileged to witness the redemption of her people from Egypt. She departed this world at a very old age and entered *Gan Eden* alive!

On this day in 5648 (1888), R' Yechiel Meir of Gustinin passed away. Born in 5576 (1816), he led a great following of Polish *chasidim* and was known as a miracle worker.

The Conditional Pardon

One stormy winter evening, a Jewish merchant found himself in Gustinin. It was already late and the houses were dark and shuttered. Alone and freezing, the merchant stood in the middle of the dark street, buffeted by a merciless wind, wondering what to do. "Where shall I go?" he asked himself silently. "Everyone is already asleep. Must I spend this frosty night out-of-doors?"

It was too cold to stand still. The stranger began pacing back and forth, when suddenly, his eyes lit up with joy. In one of the houses at the end of the street he could see a faint light. "I'll go there and see if I can find shelter for the night," he thought.

He was soon standing at the doorway of that house. The owner answered his knock and ushered him in with a friendly smile. "Welcome! You are surely looking for a place to spend the night," he said warmly.

"As a matter of fact, I am," the stranger replied gratefully. "But I am also very hungry. Could I have something to eat?"

The host, who was none other than the famous R' Yechiel Meir of Gustinin, hurried to fulfill the visitor's request. He brought some shnaps and cake to the table and urged his guest to eat his fill.

After he had finished eating, the man said that he was still hungry. His host went looking for something else to serve, but all he could find was some uncooked cereal. R' Yechiel Meir put it on the stove and began stirring it. He saw some butter on a dish and put that into the pot. When the cereal was ready, he filled up a bowl and brought it to the table for his hungry guest. The man ate bowlful after bowlful until he was sated.

"Fine! Now it is time to sleep," said the host, and he prepared his own bed for the visitor. The weary traveler sank onto it and, without even removing his muddy boots, fell into a deep sleep.

R' Yechiel Meir remained awake for the remainder of the evening since he had no bed to sleep on. When the family rose the next morning, he warned them not to make any noise so as not to awaken their guest. "He is so tired; let him sleep."

The stranger slept on. Meanwhile, R' Yechiel Meir went off to the synagogue for his morning prayers.

When the traveler finally woke up, he, too, went to the synagogue. After his prayers, he struck up a conversation with one of the local inhabitants and described where he had passed the night.

"Do you know in whose house you slept?" people said. "That was the home of the famous *tzaddik*, R' Yechiel Meir. He was the one who troubled himself for your comfort."

The man's face fell. How had he dared intrude upon the great man and cause him so much bother? And how had he let himself sleep on the *tzaddik*'s bed without realizing that there was no spare bed in the house?

Very perturbed, the man returned to R' Yechiel Meir's house and apologized. "*Rabbenu*," he said, "please forgive me for having inconvenienced you, putting you to such trouble. Forgive me for having slept in your very own bed . . . I didn't know where I was . . ."

"I will not accept any apology!" R' Yechiel Meir said.

The merchant begged and pleaded, excusing himself many times over. But the rabbi stubbornly refused. "I will not accept your excuses and explanations unless you promise me one thing."

"I will agree to anything the rabbi asks!" the merchant said with fervor.

"Then you must promise that whenever you pass through this city, Gustinin, you will come and be my guest again."

When the *tzaddik* saw the look of surprise on the merchant's face, he added, "When, do you think, I ever get a chance to fulfill my obligation of hospitality as I did last night? Do you wish to ruin my *mitzvah*?"

Indeed, from that time on, the merchant made a point of keeping his end of the bargain. Each time his business took him through Gustinin, he would stop off at the rabbi's house and avail himself of the *tzaddik*'s hospitality.

On this day in 5619 (1859), R' Menachem Mendel of Kotzk passed away. He was one of the foremost chasidic leaders, highly esteemed by all.

The Boy Who Did Not Forget

The home of R' Mendel, the Saraf of Kotzk, was like a magnet for *chasidim*. There, people forgot all of their worldly problems. There, no one paid attention to an outworn garment, a torn shoe. Only one thing mattered at the *Rebbe's* — the holy Torah! When they were in the presence of the *Rebbe*, the evil inclination — the *yetzer hara* — did not have a chance!

One of the favored *chasidim*, R' Yitzchak Meir of Gur, author of *Chidushei HaRim*, was totally immersed in study. Standing by his side was his little grandson who later became the famous R' Yehudah Aryeh Leib of Ger, the *Sefas Emes*. With round, child's eyes, full of wonder and curiosity, the little boy studied his grandfather, all the other *chasidim*, and, of course, the Kotzker *Rebbe* himself.

The small figure surrounded by all those adults aroused astonishment. What was this child doing in the Kotzker *beis medrash*? Why had R' Yitzchak Meir brought him? Everyone else had left their children and grandchildren at home, where they belonged.

As the little boy watched the studying scholars all about him, he heard a voice. It was the *rebbetzin*. "Where are my candlesticks? I have been looking for them for a long time! Where have they disappeared to? It seems as if they were swallowed up. Why, just yesterday a silver spoon was missing and last week I couldn't find my silk handkerchiefs. What is going on here?"

He could hear the *shammash's* reply. "And is it a wonder that all those items disappear? This is an open house. People come and go freely. Everything is *hefker*, unguarded, as if there were no owner."

"*Hefker?*" A voice joined in from the *beis medrash*. It was the *Rebbe*, himself, who had heard the conversation from behind the closed door. Nothing escaped him. "*Hefker?*" he thundered. "And why should things be different? Who needs to put silver and valuables under lock and key when the Torah specifically says, 'Thou shalt not steal'?"

The little boy looked at the *Rebbe* and suddenly felt as if the house where he was staying, the home of the Saraf of Kotzk, was surrounded by a thick, high wall built of the words *'lo signov* — thou shalt not steal'. And this wall moved outwards, on and on until it encompassed the entire world, preventing anyone from taking that which was not his!

The boy never forgot the roar of the Kotzker *Rebbe's Lo signov*. When he became the *Rebbe* of tens of thousands of *chasidim*, that roar continued to echo in his ears and the mighty wall of those two words, which he had pictured as a child, remained vivid in his mind's eye.

On this day in 5654 (1894), R' Yehoshua of Belz passed away. R' Yehoshua, who was born in 5585 (1825), was the leader of thousands of Belzer *chasidim*. He established the *Machzikei Hadas* organization in Galicia and managed all the Jewish affairs in that country. But aside from his concern for the public welfare, he was also involved with the plight of the individual *chasid* and his problems.

No Room for Compromise

R' Yehoshua of Belz once had to go to Lvov for business connected with the *Machzikei Hadas* organization which he had founded. Upon this occasion he met a Reform Jew who asked him, "Why do you fight against us? Would it not be better if we reached a peaceful compromise?"

R' Yehoshua replied, "When one person sues another for ten thousand rubles and the latter refuses to pay — there is room for a compromise. He may agree to receive half or a third of the sum and forget the rest.

"But we Jews have six hundred and thirteen commandments, all of which are holy and precious to us. We do not want, nay, we cannot, discard or surrender even one. Where, then, is there room for compromise?"

Not to Die but to Live

A chasid once came to R' Yehoshua of Belz and asked, "Rebbe, help me to die as an honest Jew!"

The tzaddik replied, "That was the very request that the wicked Bilaam made when he said, 'Let my soul die the death of the righteous' (*Bamidbar 23:10*). Bilaam was happy to live as a gentile and indulge himself, but when it came to dying, he wished the honorable death of a Jew. But we Jews should strive to *live* as Jews!"

24 Shevat

On this day *Hashem* spoke comforting words to Zecharyah *Hanavi* about Jerusalem. Even in later generations, when we no longer have prophecy, our sages nevertheless were blessed with *Ruach HaKodesh* (Divine inspiration).

Twenty-Two Additional Years

E ach night, about midnight, R' Avraham Halevi Beruchim, of Tsefas, would awaken and wander through the streets, weeping. He would call out the names of the scholars of Tsefas and would repeat them until he saw them leaving their homes.

Then, at midnight, a medley of sounds rose up into the night air: The chanting of the *gemara* mingled with the sing-song of the *mishnah*; chapters of *Zohar* and *Midrash* were interwoven with one another in a sweet melody; psalms, chapters of *Neviim*, prayers and *techinah* requests enveloped Tsefas.

And all this in the merit of R' Avraham Halevi Beruchim, in whom, the Ari *Hakadosh* averred, the soul of Yirmiyahu *Hanavi* had been reborn.

The Ari once summoned R' Avraham and said, "Your days are completed; your life has reached its end. Nevertheless, I can see that there is some slight hope for you through a *tikkun*, a special act or penance which can grant you an additional twenty-two years."

"What must I do?" R' Avraham asked.

"I see," the Ari replied, "that you must go up to Jerusalem. There, by the Western Wall, you must pour out your heart in prayer. If you succeed in appeasing the Almighty and are granted a glimpse of the *Shechinah*, the Divine Presence, you will live another twenty-two years."

R' Avraham hastened to travel up to Jerusalem. For three days and three nights he fasted, not tasting even a drop of water. Throughout this time he was sunken in prayer and pleading. On the third day he went to the *Kosel Hamaaravi* and there, continued with his tearful prayer.

Suddenly, he raised his eyes and saw the *Shechinah* resting upon the stones of the Wall. He fell prostrate with a shriek and wept until he fainted.

In his swoon he dreamt he saw the *Shechinah* again. The *Shechinah* wiped away his tears and said to him, "Be comforted, Avraham, my son, for there is hope for you. 'Sons will return to their border for I shall gather in their captivities and have mercy on them'."

R' Avraham awoke and returned to Tsefas in uplifted spirits.

When the Ari saw him, he said, "I see that you have, indeed, beheld the Divine Presence. I am certain that you will live for another twenty-two years."

And so it was. Twenty-two years later R' Avraham Halevi Beruchim was summoned to the Heavenly Academy, the *yeshivah shel maalah*.

On this day, in 5521 (1761), R' Shabsai, father of R' Yisrael of Kozhnitz, passed away. This unknown *tzaddik* was privileged to have a son who enlightened the world with his Torah teachings.

The Dance that Reached Heaven

R' Shabsai eked out a meager existence as a bookbinder, earning only pennies to support himself and his wife. He, often, did not even have dry bread to put on his table. Yet he and his wife refused to accept charity. "We shall make do with what we have," they would reassure one another and be happy in their lot.

One thing, however, disturbed their contentment. They had

not been granted children. They prayed long and hard and even when they reached old age, did not despair of being thus blessed.

One week R' Shabsai had not earned as much as one penny! Not only did they starve on the weekdays — and they were already accustomed to this — but this time they would not have anything with which to buy *Shabbos* provisions.

Friday came and the house was bare. Poverty cried out from every corner — from the table bare of wine or *challos*, from the candlesticks without their candles, from the pantry which did not contain even a crumb.

"*Shabbos* is approaching," R' Shabsai's wife noted sadly, "and we have nothing with which to greet and honor it."

"Then we will fast!" replied her husband. "We will fast this *Shabbos* rather than accept charity."

His wife nodded humbly in agreement. Her look followed R' Shabsai as he left the house that Friday afternoon, earlier than usual, to go to the synagogue.

That evening, R' Shabsai waited for the last worshiper to leave before he started on his way home. He did not want to see the townspeople's reaction when they passed his house and saw that it was dark. He did not want to answer their questions or to parry their pitying glances. He did not want their kind offers of help which he knew they would extend when they heard his story. "No, not their sympathy nor their food," he thought as he walked along, very slowly.

When he reached the turn of the road from where he could see his cottage, he drew back in surprise. The house which should have been dark was all lit up! He could see the lights of the *Shabbos* candles dancing. But the light did not gladden his heart. On the contrary, it was twisted with pain. R' Shabsai suspected that his wife had weakened and borrowed some candles from a neighbor.

When he entered his house, another surprise awaited him;

the table was set for the meal, complete with wine and *challos*, while the aroma of fish and meat was undeniable.

R' Shabsai's sorrow grew sevenfold. All this bounty must have come from kind neighbors — how could it be otherwise? Not wishing to grieve his wife and spoil her joy, he refrained from asking any questions.

"You are surely wondering at the sight of the candles, wine and all the other foods on the table," she said, discerning R' Shabsai's unspoken displeasure. "Know that *Hashem*'s salvation comes with the winking of an eye!"

"What do you mean?" he asked.

"Let me tell you what happened. When you left for the *beis knesses*, I decided that if I did not have any food to cook or other preparations to make in honor of the *Shabbos*, at least I would give the house a thorough scouring. I turned the house upside-down banishing every speck of dirt and dust. And then, in a hidden corner, I noticed a pair of old gloves. I was about to throw them away when I noticed several golden buttons sewn on them. I ripped them off and ran to sell them. I got a lot of money for them, too, enough to buy all the provisions which you see before you. So now you know where the food and candles come from. You see, I did not beg or borrow from neighbors, as you first suspected."

"Blessed is He and blessed is His Name!" R' Shabsai cried out aloud, his face beaming. "Heaven has sent us our salvation so that we need not profane the *Shabbos* by treating it like a weekday!" And so saying, R' Shabsai's feet lifted him up and he began dancing about with wild enthusiasm, thanking *Hashem* for His great kindness.

❧   ❧   ❧

In faraway Mezibuz, the Baal Shem Tov sat at the table with his *chasidim* when suddenly, without warning, he began laughing.

The disciples looked at him in wonder. What was the *Rebbe* laughing about? And why in the middle of the meal? But no one dared ask him.

Only after *havdalah* did one of the favored disciples, R' Zev Kitzis, summon up the courage to say, "*Rebbe*, we are all wondering why you laughed last night halfway through the meal."

Instead of replying, the Baal Shem Tov told him to have the driver prepare the carriage for a trip. The *talmidim* were also asked to join him. Driver and disciples were already accustomed to such journeys of unrevealed destination. All questions, they were sure, would be duly answered.

The wheels devoured the miles for hour upon hour. Towards morning they reached Apta. "Summon R' Shabsai the bookbinder," ordered the Baal Shem Tov.

When the bookbinder arrived, the *tzaddik* said, "Tell us, what happened in your home this Friday night?"

R' Shabsai spoke of his poverty and told them how he and his loyal wife had decided to fast on *Shabbos* rather than accept charity. "However, we did not have to fast, after all. For a miracle happened!" he exclaimed happily. And he described how his wife had found the golden buttons and sold them to buy provisions. "I was so thrilled," he continued, "and my heart was so overflowing with gratitude that I broke out spontaneously into a fervent dance to express my great joy and give thanks to *Hashem*."

"Know," the Baal Shem Tov said to him, "that your joy reached all the way to Heaven. All the hosts of Heaven joined you in your happiness. Now," he turned to his disciples, "do you understand why I laughed during the meal?"

R' Shabsai stared at them in surprise. The Baal Shem Tov continued, "And now, R' Shabsai, you are being rewarded by being allowed one request. What shall it be?"

"Surely not riches," answered R' Shabsai. "There is only

one thing that I lack to make my happiness complete and that is a son. My wife and I are already old, but have not, yet, been blessed with children."

"So be it."

The Baal Shem Tov blessed them and *Hashem* fulfilled that blessing. By the end of the year, R' Shabsai and his wife were enriched with a son!

The Baal Shem Tov himself attended the child's *bris* and was honored as *sandak*. The child was named Yisrael since he had been born through the blessing of R' Yisrael Baal Shem Tov.

The bookbinder's son grew up to become wise and saintly. He eventually became known as the famous R' Yisrael of Kozhnitz.

R' Yisrael of Kozhnitz (born in 5497, or 1737, passed away on the fourteenth of *Tishrei* 5575, or 1816) was one of the leaders of *Chasidism* whose wisdom illuminated the world.

On this day in 5427 (1667), R' David Halevi Segal, the *Taz*, named from his work, *Turei Zahav*, passed away. The *Taz* was one of the great *poskim* upon whose decisions we rely to this very day.

He Did Not Benefit from the Crown of Torah

*I*n the years of 5408-09 (1648-49), known as '*Tach veTat*', the Cossacks wreaked havoc upon the Jewish communities of Europe. They plundered and murdered, annihilating entire Jewish communities.

The Cossack pogroms caused many Jews to flee for their lives, forsaking their homes and cities to wander helplessly, constantly on the go, seeking some temporary shelter from the ravagers.

R' David Halevi, the *Taz*, was forced to leave Ostrov, where he served as rabbi. He and his family eventually reached Lvov, Poland, and settled there.

No one in the city dreamed that the father of this impoverished family, which had come from afar and taken up residence in a dilapidated hovel, was one of the leaders of the generation! No one even bothered to ask where he had come from.

They did see, however, that the head of this bedraggled

family studied assiduously in the Lvov *beis medrash*, day and night. Sometimes, people would try to glean some information from him, but his answers were brief and he went right back to his study.

The women of Lvov tried to make the acquaintance of the mother of this new family, but they were not very successful. They did notice that, from time to time, she would go to the pawnshop to sell an article of jewelry or some silver household item.

The family needed help and the charity treasurers in the city offered their assistance to R' David. But he was not interested.

They approached his wife and asked if she wanted any financial assistance from the community.

Tears flooded her eyes at the question. "But we are not beggars, G-d forbid," she replied, trying to hide how offended she was by the question. Unable to check her tears, she blurted out, "We do not want charity, but if you could find some work for my husband for a few hours a day, leaving him enough time for his studies, we would be most grateful."

A suitable position was soon found. A supervisor of *nikur* (removal of forbidden fats and tendons) was needed at the slaughterhouse. Since R' David studied Torah day and night, it was assumed that he was qualified. His name was suggested and, after he was tested in the necessary *halachos*, R' David was given the appointment.

But this did not bring an end to the family's troubles.

Some of the senior *shochtim* in the city looked askance at the installation of a newcomer to such an important position and felt that one of them should have been chosen. They schemed to have him removed and an opportunity soon presented itself.

Once, when cattle were being slaughtered, the *shochtim*

ruled that a certain animal was *treife*. R' David ruled that they were mistaken — the animal was perfectly kosher.

A heated argument arose. Finally, the *shochtim* went to the rabbi of the city, R' Meir Zak, and presented the facts of the matter.

R' Meir listened to their arguments, then heard the supervisor's opinion but in the end ruled the animal to be *treife*. The *Taz* was dissatisfied. He repeated his arguments and proofs to the contrary, but he was not heeded.

"Then I will bring some additional proofs that the animal is kosher," he insisted, and left the court.

Just then a young boy passed by, carrying a wrapped package. "What do you have there, child?" the *Taz* asked.

"I have a slaughtered chicken here which the rabbi just examined," he replied.

"What was the problem?"

"I don't know. My mother sent me to R' Meir with this chicken. He examined it and said it was *treife*."

"Show it to me," said the *Taz*. The boy removed the wrapping. The *Taz* poked at the chicken and finally said, "Go back to R' Meir and tell him to look up what it says in *Yoreh Deah, Hilchos Trefos*, section such-and-such, and in the *Taz*, paragraph so-and-so."

The boy rewrapped the chicken and returned to the rabbi's study, delivering the *Taz's* message word for word.

R' Meir took the bird and placed it on the table. Suddenly he realized that, indeed, a law had slipped his mind, a law which also applied to the animal which he had a short while before ruled as *treife*, against the judgment of the supervisor.

R' Meir was great enough to acknowledge his mistake. He was troubled that he had been so severe towards R' David, the supervisor, who must be a great scholar.

"Call R' David back," he said to his *shammash*.

R' David soon arrived. The two men now entered into a

scholarly discussion. It did not take long for R' Meir Zak to realize that the man before him was a very uncommon exalted individual.

"Why do you conceal your greatness?" the rabbi of Lvov asked.

The *Taz* replied, "Our Sages taught that 'whoever takes advantage of the crown of Torah is uprooted from this world.' Besides, there was no need ..."

R' David rose to leave but R' Meir detained him. Then he told his *shammash* to fetch the leaders of the community.

Upon their arrival, he said, "Know that the man before us, who is employed as the supervisor of the slaughterhouse, is a most unique personality, a man fit to serve as rabbi of the city. I hereby hand in my resignation so that he can replace me, for he is more deserving."

They were stunned. R' David, who was at the center of the affair, turned pale. Trembling with fear, he said, "My honored sirs, I am but dust under the feet of R' Meir. Who am I to take his place in his lifetime?"

R' Meir was adamant. "But I am already very old and feeble. My eyes are weak and my vigor has waned. I no longer have the strength to lead this community properly. And now that *Hashem* has brought before me a man full of the spirit of G-d, a man in his prime who can grapple with the daily problems of a community, it is only proper that he occupy the seat of the rabbinate, since he is better suited and qualified."

They saw that R' Meir was speaking from the depths of his heart and that his words were wise and logical. And so they appointed R' David Halevi Segal, the *Taz*, as the *av beis din* of Lvov.

A few years later, when R' Meir was called to his eternal rest, the *Taz* was officially appointed as the rabbi of the congregation and head of the illustrious *yeshivah* in Lvov.

On the evening of this day, the eve of the twenty-eighth of *Shevat*, in 5697 (1937), the saintly R' Menachem Nachum Twersky of Rachmistrivka passed away. R' Menachem Nachum was born in Russia in 5600 (1840) to his holy father, R' Yochanan. He was named for his grandfather, author of *Meor Einayim*, and was highly esteemed by thousands of *chasidim* while still a young man. Towards the end of his days he went up to *Eretz Yisrael* and settled in Jerusalem.

The Promissory Note that Went up in Flames

*I*n a tiny Russian village, where rooftops were buried under layers of snow for most of the year and where the trees were always bowed and shrouded by their thick white blankets, there lived a merchant who was a *chasid* of R' Nachum. After his marriage, he tried his hand at peddling. Foundering through the perpetual snow, he would travel to the neighboring hamlets with his small pack of goods, trying to eke out a few pennies for his livelihood.

His family grew and luck was with him. His peddler's pack became a chain of stores which flourished into a big business with many connections.

But expansion required capital. And so he turned to a wealthy gentile neighbor who agreed to lend him a large sum of money at a reasonable rate of interest, payable upon a certain date. The transaction was duly recorded and signed.

But from that time on, fortune frowned upon the Jew and instead of expanding, his business began plummeting downwards until he was forced to sell out. He was reduced to poverty.

And if these troubles were not enough, the gentile creditor began to demand the return of his money. Day in and day out he would remind the Jew that the interest was growing. The Jew lived in terror, feeling as if this debt with its interest was sucking up the very marrow of his bones. All his lovely dreams of riches and status were a thing of the past. The present was a bitter reality.

When every item of value had been sold, the Jew saw that he had just enough to pay back the principal and the interest to the gentile. But in his confusion, he forgot to demand the document of the loan in return for the payment. And so, it remained in the gentile's possession.

The gentile took full advantage of this oversight and began demanding payment all over again.

Reduced to utter poverty, the Jew was beside himself. He did not know what to do or where to turn. In his despair, he did what so many others do — they turn to the anchor of hope, the haven in time of distress — the *Rebbe*. The *Rebbe* of Rachmistrivka had an open door for all and a heart big enough to contain all the sorrows of his *chasidim*, whom he loved, consoled, advised and encouraged.

The businessman had been trying to hide his condition from the *Rebbe* for some time, but now he had no choice. Even if he were able to resign himself to poverty, he was still not rid of that dreadful debt which the gentile was claiming for a second time. And there was nothing that he could do about it!

The *chasid* feared that he was liable to do something drastic; he might murder the gentile.

He came to the *Rebbe* and, in a sea of tears, unburdened his troubled heart. He described his desperate situation — his poverty, but spoke mainly about the debt that the gentile still claimed from him.

When he had finished, his heavy sighs still echoed in the room. The Rebbe looked at the broken man before him and seemed to caress him with his gentle, caring look. He comforted him in a soft voice and finally said, "Go out and buy some shnaps and *Hashem* will help!"

Bewildered and confused, the man was not sure that he had heard correctly. How did one solve such weighty problems with a bottle of whiskey? But the Rebbe's beaming face exuded confidence and reassurance, so much so, that the trusting *chasid* refused to question his judgment.

He borrowed some money from a friend and went out to buy a bottle of the strongest shnaps he could find and returned home, his heart brimming with hope and trust that *Hashem*'s salvation would come in a twinkling of the eye.

Feeling exuberantly happy, moved by some hidden impulse, upon his return home he sent a note to his creditor telling him to come and fetch the money.

The gentile could hardly believe his eyes. He felt like a warrior returning from battle crowned with victory. He put on his finest clothing and, his eyes gleaming with joy at the prospect of the easily won money, he set off for the Jew's home. Nor did he forget to bring along the document this time, feeling that he had milked the Jew enough. Why, the interest on the original loan was itself an enormous sum.

The Jew welcomed him with a smile and invited him to sit down. He poured a full glass of shnaps for the gentile and handed it to him. The gentile downed it with appreciation. This was excellent stuff! He now took the liberty to pour

himself another glassful, and then, another, all the while praising the fine spirits. He drank like one possessed until he had drained the bottle of its very last drop.

The gentile was weaving drunkenly back and forth, a dazed look in his eyes. The strong whiskey had altogether dulled his senses and he could no longer tell his left hand from his right.

His bleary eyes saw the empty bottle on the table and he began shouting hoarsely, "Hey, Moshke, stop up the bottle. That precious shnaps will evaporate. Put the top on, I say!"

While shouting, he put his hand into his pocket, fished out the first piece of paper which he found and stuffed up the mouth of the bottle with it.

The paper ... the very paper which had caused "Moshke" such heartache and tears ...

The paper which had caused him despair and depression, sleepless nights and haunted days — the promissory note — was now the stopper of the empty bottle.

The drunken man raised himself heavily from his chair and reeled over to the door, apologizing thickly that he was very tired and would return for his money on the morrow.

The door slammed shut.

The *chasid* got up from his chair and went to fill his pipe in order to calm his pounding heart and whirling thoughts. He lit it and suddenly, the note stopping up the empty bottle caught fire; it was reduced to a pinch of ashes.

The *chasid* took a plain sheet of paper and stuffed it into the mouth of the bottle, lest the gentile return immediately.

Early the next morning, there was a knocking at the *chasid's* door. A now sober creditor entered and his eyes darted nervously about, looking for the empty bottle and its paper stopper.

There it rested on the table. He lunged for it. But he found only a blank sheet of paper.

He now understood that the G-d of the Jews had come to the debtor's aid in his time of need. He did not mention anything about the note, just mumbled something under his breath and left abashed. There was nothing to say; he no longer had a claim upon the Jew, nothing that would hold up in any court.

The *chasid* went to the window, looked out towards Rachmistrivka, as if seeking some invisible point in the distance. Snowflakes fluttered slowly down upon the window-panes as he thought to himself how deep and penetrating was the vision of the *tzaddik* who had given him such good advice and who had known the wonderful connection between a bottle of shnaps and a promissory note . . .

During the time of the Talmud, this day was celebrated as a *yom tov* for it commemorated the day that Antiochus died. He had passed harsh laws against the Jews. It reminded the people that while every generation has villains who seek to annihilate Jewry, *Hashem* foils their plots and rescues us from their clutches.

A Question of Life and Death

A delegation of ministers came to the Egyptian sultan asking for a private audience. "We have something very secret to divulge to Your Majesty," they whispered.

"What is it?"

"It is common knowledge that you especially favor your Jewish physician and praise him always. But there is one thing that Your Majesty does not know," said the spokesman in measured words.

He paused to study the sultan's face.

"Say what you have to say!" the sultan ordered.

The minister lowered his voice confidentially, "We have come here to warn you that your beloved physician is seeking to assassinate you."

Silence gripped the air. The sultan looked at the others and they nodded knowingly. So, they knew something that he was not aware of! His face reddened with fury. "Can it be? Here, in my very palace and under my very nose?" He pounded the table with his fist. "Bring him here at once and he will be tried."

The royal physician, R' Moshe ben Maimon — the Rambam, was summoned and a quick trial was held. But when the time came to pass sentence, the sultan felt that he could not outright kill the man he had come to trust and love.

The Rambam had been accused of a plot to assassinate the sultan. This was treason, punishable by death. But the sultan could not erase all the years of faithful service which the Rambam had given him or forget the many times that he had actually saved his life. How could he have this man hanged?

The sultan was unable to directly sentence the Rambam to death. He would give him one last chance. He announced that on the following day the Rambam's fate would be decided by lots. A special box would be prepared containing two pieces of paper, one marked 'life' and the other — 'death'. The Rambam would seal his own fate by drawing one of the two lots. If he chose 'life', he would be allowed to live, if 'death', justice would be served and he would have chosen his own death.

One of the sultan's clerks was charged with preparing the lots. He secretly exulted at being given this responsibility, since he was a rabid anti-Semite. As he was preparing them, he was struck by a brilliant plan; he would make the two notes identical, both bearing the word 'death'! The Rambam would die, no matter which lot he selected.

He was so thrilled with his clever idea that he decided to hold a party that evening. He invited all of his friends and acquaintances and when his spirits were high with wine and good food, he became careless and boasted of his stroke of genius which would assure the Rambam's death. His friends, who similarly envied and despised the Jew, gloated together with him.

The courtroom was packed the next day. The sultan was there as were all the ministers. As the Rambam stood there, stately and impressive as always, someone came over to him and whispered in his ear, "I am certain that you will die!"

The Rambam detected a note of hatred and disdain in the voice. The statement set him thinking. "How could that man be so certain that I will die? Maybe the lots have been tampered with. Probably both notes have the same word, 'death', written on them."

These thoughts raced through his head with lightning speed when a brilliant idea struck him. He turned to the man and said evenly, "And I am certain that I will live!"

The ballot box was brought in. It contained two slips of paper. The court clerk stood up and announced: "The accused is requested to step forward and withdraw one of the two ballots."

The Rambam inserted his hand into the box and selected a note. Without glancing at it, he thrust it into his mouth and swallowed it! Then he turned to the spectators and said, "You all saw that the box contained two notes. One of them bore the word 'life' and the other 'death'. I took one note and swallowed it. Let us examine the remaining note. If it says 'life', then the note I chose must have said 'death' and that is to be my fate. If, however, it says 'death', this means that the one which I swallowed was the note saying 'life'."

The remaining note was removed and held up for all to see. It plainly bore the word 'death'.

"Free him!" exclaimed the sultan. "He is granted life by his own hand."

The Rambam was exonerated. He left the court with the baleful stares of his enemies boring into his back. They were furious that he had again thwarted their nefarious plot. He had outwitted them once more.

Later, the sultan called the Rambam to him and said, "Tell me, why did you swallow the note?"

The Rambam explained, "I understood what my enemies had planned for me. These are the same enemies who slandered me and told you that I sought to kill you."

When the sultan heard this, he opened an investigation which led to the imprisonment of the evil ministers.

"How great is the G-d of the Jews!" he exclaimed to the Rambam. "He implanted great wisdom in the hearts of those who fear Him, wisdom which protects and preserves them from all harm. And this brings justice to light!"

The Sign of the Fish

There once lived in Poland a Jew who rented a tavern from a squire who was a wealthy landowner. The Jew also had fishing rights to one of the lakes which his landlord owned. He paid a fixed yearly rent for his tavern, but had to give the squire half of each catch in exchange for the fishing permit. And if he only caught one fish, it rightfully belonged to the landowner.

The Jew was a simple, uneducated fellow, but honest to the core. He fulfilled the terms of the agreement to the letter and thereby earned the squire's implicit respect.

Once, on the day before *Purim*, the Jew went fishing. He sank line after line into the water but did not hook any fish. The fish evaded his bait, as if they had made a pact between themselves that his *Purim* dinner be 'fishless'. The Jew was perturbed. A *Purim* feast without fish was inconceivable! Fish was the *mazal* sign of the month of *Adar*.

It was getting late and the man was about to return home

empty handed. He began hauling in the line when, suddenly, there was a tug. He had hooked a large fish, the size of which he had not seen for a long time! He thanked *Hashem* for this wonderful gift. Now he would have a fine fish on his table for *Purim*, after all. He rowed towards shore with all his might in order to reach home in time.

As he was rowing, however, he realized that this fish really belonged to the squire who owned the lake. That was the agreement; if he went fishing and caught only one fish, he had to give it to the landlord. What a pity, he thought. He was no better off than if he had caught nothing at all! He mulled it over. Why did the landlord need a fish, after all? Did he celebrate *Purim*? He could have fish whenever he wanted. But he, the Jew, celebrated *Purim* only once a year and he *had* to have fish on his table!

To surrender the fish or to keep it, that was the question. In the end, he decided to have the fish cooked for his *Purim* feast and get his landlord a double share the next time.

But Heaven had, apparently, decreed that this fish, his precious catch, was destined to cause him much aggravation. The delectable smell of the fat fish simmering in the pot wafted all the way to a gentile neighbor's nose. He suspected that the Jew had not given his due to the landlord and went and informed on him.

The landlord fumed. He immediately sent his servant to fetch the Jew. When the tenant stood before him, the squire shouted at him, "You caught a fish in my lake today, didn't you?"

"Yes, sir," the Jew replied tremblingly.

"You cheated me out of my just due, didn't you? You concealed the fact from me and kept the fish for yourself!"

"G-d forbid! I would not cheat you. I have never cheated you before and I hope to remain loyal to you in the future," he said. He then told him all about the miracle of *Purim* and how

Jews celebrated their salvation from the clutches of the wicked Haman with a festive meal.

"I know all about the story of *Purim*," the landlord interrupted him. "In fact, I have even eaten *hamantaschen* in my life and found the prune and poppy-seed pastries very tasty. But what does that have to do with my fish?"

"Please let me explain," the Jew begged. "*Purim* comes just once a year and we are commanded to invite many guests, especially poor people, to a sumptuous feast. Now tell me, sir, what feast is complete without fish? Besides, fish happens to be the sign of the month ..." he said, explaining as best he could about the *mazal* of *Adar*.

The squire's curiosity was aroused. "What do you mean by sign?" The Jew told him about the twelve Hebrew months and their different signs of the zodiac which represented each month. The sign of the month of *Adar*, fish, reminds us of Divine Providence. "Just as the eyes of the fish never shut, so is the eye of *Hashem*, as it were, always open and alert to protect us," he added. "G-d looks after us in our difficult exile and shields us from the schemes of our enemies."

"That is all fine and well. But what does it have to do with the fish that you caught and that rightfully belongs to me?" the landlord persisted.

"The matter is very simple, sir. You see, I only caught this one fish and thought that G-d had sent it especially to grace my table. As for you, I intended to pay you back with an extra fish I catch at some other time. I will give it to you when I go fishing again."

"Very well," said the landlord. "This time you are forgiven. But if it happens again, I will skin you alive ..."

Some time later, the Polish nobility held a national conference. Counts, barons, dukes, large and small landowners all gathered to discuss government policies in their mutual interests. The conversation turned to Jews, who were often the tenants and managers of the large estates. Each landowner began complaining about his 'Jew' taking advantage of him. One told how a Jew had bargained him down, another said that a Jew had forced him to give lumber rights of an entire forest for half price. "Our" squire told the story of how he had been cheated out of a fish. Each one had his personal story of imagined injustice. The Polish noblemen became so enraged against the Jews that they decided to pass a law banishing all Jews from Polish holdings.

They worked out a text for the new law and passed it around to be signed. But before the first nobleman had a chance to sign it, the door opened and in walked an elegantly dressed aristocrat. Gold and diamonds sparkled on his blue and purple attire. All eyes were riveted on him. The entire gathering rose, as one, and bowed towards the newcomer. They showed him to a chair at the head of the table and honored him to be the first to sign the bill.

The nobleman read the document with interest, then said, "I think that you are mistaken, my friends. Your arguments are petty and self defeating. What will happen if you evict the Jews from your properties? Will gentile caretakers do a better job? Are you not familiar with our Polish peasants? All they know is how to get drunk. They will let your lands go to ruin. Your new managers will pile up debts instead of showing profits, as the Jews do. Believe me, there are no better tenants than Jews." So saying, he swept up the document and ripped it to shreds. Then he bowed and walked out of the room.

The assembled nobility sat there spellbound. No one knew the identity of the impressive-looking nobleman and all of them were ashamed to admit it. Slowly, they emerged from their trance and without a word, dispersed.

The landlord of our story was especially abashed once he realized what a reckless thing he had been about to do. The only complaint he had against his faithful tenant was that one incident with the fish and that certainly was not a valid reason to evict him, especially when he knew that he would never find anyone as good to replace him. But he could not help being curious about the anonymous nobleman who had torn up the bill and broken up the meeting. He summoned up his courage and said to a friend, "I am really embarrassed to ask, but I am very curious to know the identity of that nobleman who destroyed the document."

"To tell you the truth," his companion confided, "I don't know who he was, either. In fact, I was about to ask you that very question."

They decided to ask the others. One after another confessed that he did not know who the stranger was. No one had ever seen him before or heard of him, either.

Upon his return, the landlord called the Jewish tenant to him and said, "Do you remember what you told me about the sign of the fish? And how your G-d watches over you with open eyes to protect you from harm? Well, I saw Him with my own eyes . . ."

He went on to tell him what had happened at that memorable meeting. When he was finished, the Jew said with a smile, "I don't believe that you actually saw my G-d, for no one can see him. But the man you describe, who was dressed in blue and purple and gold trimming — that could only have been Mordechai of the *Purim* chronicle who came especially to save us Jews from a terrible decree. This must be in the merit of our *Purim* feast. So you see, the *mazal* of the fish stood by us this time, after all!"

This is *erev rosh chodesh*. Our Sages said that the month of *Adar* ushers in joy because of the miracle of *Purim* which took place in this month.

Why Adar?

W hen Haman sought to destroy the Jews, he first decided to examine each month of the Jewish calendar to see which was best suited for his evil scheme.

He began with *Nisan*, but this did not find favor in his eyes, since it had the Festival of Passover, when Jews celebrate their redemption from bondage. This was too favorable for them.

The month of *Iyar* did not seem suitable, because it had the Festival of *Pesach Sheni* and, besides, on the fifteenth of this month the manna began falling to sustain the Jews in the desert. "This cannot be propitious," he decided, and discarded *Iyar*.

Sivan was not to be considered, since this was the month of the Giving of the Torah.

Tammuz and *Av* were next in line. These two months came before the Almighty and said, "Master of the world, are the tragedies which fall in our months not enough? The wall of Jerusalem was breached in *Tammuz* while the *Beis Hamikdash* was burned in *Av*. And these are only some of the misfortunes which overtook the Jews in this season!" *Hashem* heard their plea and prevented Haman from executing his decree at that time.

He did not find *Elul* suitable, either, for in this month Jews observed the commandment of *maaser beheimah*, setting aside one tenth of their newborn flocks. (*Rosh Chodesh Elul* marks the new year's counting of *maaser beheimah*.) This would be weighed in their merit.

And the following month, *Tishrei*, was altogether out of the question since it was overflowing with *mitzvos* and merits for the Jewish people: *shofar, Yom Kippur, succah, arbaah minim*. Haman realized that at once.

Sarah *Imenu* passed away in the month of *Cheshvan* (as did Rachel). And Sarah's passing was a reminder of the *akeidah* whose merit has protected the Jewish people throughout history.

Kislev was next. This was not a good month because of the merit of *Chanukah* which Jews would observe in years to come.

Haman shied away from *Teves*, as well, for in this month Ezra would pass strict regulations weeding out all the gentiles from the Jewish community and making safeguards to prevent assimilation.

Shevat was not likely because the Jews had fought the war over the murder of the 'concubine of Givah' and destroyed the idol of Michah.

He had now reached *Adar*, the twelfth month, and could find no special merit which protected the Jews at this time. He rejoiced and said, "Jews do not have good luck in this month, besides which, it is the month in which Moshe their Prophet passed away." Little did Haman realize that Moshe *Rabbenu* was also born in this month. This would stand Israel in good stead!

Haman saw that *Adar*'s *mazal* sign was a fish, and he said,

"Just as fish devour one another, so shall I devour Israel!"

But *Hashem* said differently: "Some fish swallow, others are swallowed up. Haman will be one who is swallowed up without swallowing others!"

And that was the wicked one's fate!

(According to *Midrash Esther Rabbah, parashah* 7)

30 Shevat

First day of Rosh Chodesh Adar. On *Rosh Chodesh Adar* of 5575 (1815), R' Avraham Shmuel Binyamin Sofer was born. The Kesav Sofer, son of the Chasam Sofer, served as rabbi of Pressburg and died on the nineteenth of *Teves*, 5632 (1872).

A Bar-Mitzvah Gift

The doctors who were huddled around the patient's bed did not utter a word, but their expressions spoke volumes of despair. There was not a glimmer of hope in anyone's eyes.

"There is nothing more to do," one of them finally sighed, pointing helplessly at the six-year-old boy lying in a coma.

"His moments are numbered. He will soon die," another agreed sadly.

The family sent for the members of the *chevrah kadisha*, the burial committee, who were accustomed to being present at the side of a dying person. They lit candles around the

R' Avraham Shmuel Binyamin Sofer

child's bed and began reciting those psalms which one recites as the soul departs.

The doctors had not yet left the room. They looked upon their patient, little Avraham Shmuel Binyamin, with pity.

One of them turned to the father, R' Moshe Sofer, the Chasam Sofer, and said in a pain-ridden voice, "There is no natural way for this child to recover. But I know that you are a holy man. Perhaps your prayers can change the course of nature and effect a miracle."

The Chasam Sofer heard this and was infused with hope. He rose, stood by the cupboard which contained the manuscripts of works he had written, and burst into a torrent of prayers.

The words flowed from his mouth. Suddenly, those standing by the boy's bedside noticed a slight improvement. His eyelids fluttered and a faint flush appeared on his white cheeks. His condition had stabilized. The *chevrah kadisha* extinguished their candles and tiptoed out of the room.

The Chasam Sofer's disciples who were present at the time heard their master saying, "My prayers have given him a reprieve of fifty years."

And so it was. R' Avraham Shmuel Binyamin Sofer lived for an additional fifty years before he was summoned to Heaven.

During his *bar-mitzvah* celebration, one of the prominent figures of the community approached the youngster and gave him an exquisite silver container.

"What kind of a box is this?" asked the boy. "What does it contain?" He opened it up and saw a few thin candles. He looked at them with questioning eyes.

The donor explained the mystery of the candles. "These are the candles which the members of the *chevrah kadisha* lit when you lay ill and dying at the age of six. *Hashem* wrought a miracle and saved your life. I now bring them to you as a gift."

R' Avraham Shmuel Binyamin grew up to become a great man and in time, was appointed as rabbi and *rosh yeshivah* of Pressburg, after his father passed away. This *yeshivah* produced thousands of excellent scholars, many of whom served as rabbis in illustrious communities throughout Europe.

Adar

Rosh Chodesh Adar. This is the month that was transformed from sorrow to joy. Jewish children took an active part in praying for their people's salvation in the time of the wicked Haman. It was their merit, in great part, that stood by the Jews in the miracle of *Purim*.

Out of the Mouths of Babes

Haman left the king's palace in high spirits, having just signed the official letters ordering the destruction of the Jewish nation. Surrounded by his friends, he strode jauntily through the streets of Shushan when he met Mordechai, trying to overtake three little boys who had just finished their studies that day.

Their curiosity aroused by this scene, Haman and his friends decided to pursue the group.

They followed behind and heard Mordechai accost the first child. "What did you learn today, my child?" he asked.

"I learned the verse in *Mishlei* which says, 'Do not fear from a sudden danger or from the approaching threat of the wicked'."

The second boy then said, "And I learned a verse from *Yeshayahu* which says, 'Take counsel — but it will be foiled; plan a plot — but it shall not be, for *Hashem* is with us'."

The third one spoke, "I also learned a verse from *Yeshayahu* which says, 'I made and I shall bear and I shall suffer and I shall rescue'."

Upon hearing these three verses, Mordechai's face lit up with joy.

Haman asked him, "What did these youngsters just tell you to make you so happy?"

Mordechai replied, "These tender students brought me good news. They told me that your plot will be foiled and that I have nothing to fear from you."

Haman grew furious. He decided that he would first kill these little boys before he attended to Mordechai. (*Yalkut Shimoni Esther 6*)

Father and Daughter

O n this day in 5423 (1663), R' Shabsai Hakohen passed away. His work, *Sifsei Kohen* on *Shulchan Aruch*, became one of the basic texts on Jewish law. The Shach was born in Lithuania in 5382 (1622).

❀ ❀ ❀

With a stomping of hobnailed boots, a clanging of spears and swords and fierce battle cries on their lips, the French soldiers stormed their way into the Jewish quarter of Austrian cities. They swept from house to house, plundering and pillaging, until the entire neighborhood looked like a bloody battleground.

"There's the rabbi's house!" one soldier shouted. With a shout of anticipation, they swung towards the house and threw themselves against the locked door. It gave way beneath their weight and they were soon inside.

"Help!" cried the woman of the house as she sank lifeless to the ground. She had died from fright.

When the rabbi quickly ascertained that there was nothing he could do for her, he took advantage of the soldier's preoccupation with the plunder and slipped outside, carrying his five-year-old daughter on his shoulders.

His feet carried him swiftly towards the forest at the outskirts of the city. "There," he thought, "I will be able to hide until this pogrom passes," and he ran with all his might.

When he was safely in the thick of the woods, he breathed with relief. But his sense of security did not last long for he could hear the battle whoops of another group of soldiers advancing towards the city through the forest. He was caught between the anvil and the hammer!

Without knowing where to turn, he ran wherever his legs carried him. His heart pounding with fear and effort, he did not even realize that his daughter had slipped off his shoulders and fallen to the ground. He continued to flee, not realizing that the swifter he ran, the more distance he put between himself and his only daughter.

R' Shabsai Hakohen, the Shach, was a victim of a war between France and his homeland, Austria. And now he had been driven away from his home.

While he was still escaping the French soldiers, a troop of them reached the spot where the little girl had fallen. "A child in the middle of the forest?" they wondered. "How did she get here?"

They reported the find to the king, who was sitting in a coach nearby. He was also amazed and told them to bring her at once.

Her face was drenched with tears when she was laid inside the royal coach. She had not stopped crying from the time she had fallen off her father's shoulders. The king tried to comfort her and finally, she stopped her weeping. "What a lovely child!" the king's escorts marveled. "She must be hungry," said the king. "Bring her something to eat."

Some food was brought, but the little girl shook her head and refused to touch it. "Why aren't you eating?" the king asked. "Aren't you hungry? Or don't you find this to your liking?"

The little girl opened her eyes and replied clearly, "I am a Jew and I must not eat food which is not kosher."

"Then give the child some fruits and vegetables," the king ordered. "Don't force her to eat anything she does not want."

The king had already decided that upon his return to the palace, he would adopt this forest foundling as a playmate for his own daughter. An only child, the princess would now have a companion her own age. The two girls could grow up as sisters.

And so it was. The two girls liked one another. They did everything together and were treated alike except in one matter: The Jewish girl refused to eat of the palace food and so, was allowed to eat what was permissible to her. All were amazed that she knew exactly what she could or could not eat.

They grew up as loving sisters, playing and studying together. One night, the Shach's daughter awoke in alarm, jumped from her bed and ran to the princess' bed. By the light of the moon she saw a snake coiled around her neck, ready to strike. But the princess was fast asleep.

The Jewish girl began screaming; she roused all of the palace servants. "Help!" she shouted. "There is a snake around the princess' neck!"

The servants came on the run; the snake was crushed to death and the princess saved.

"All thanks to you!" said the king and queen to the little

Jewish girl. And after that dreadful night, she became even more cherished in the palace.

Time passed and the girls grew. A tutor was brought to educate the princess. The girls enjoyed their lessons and studied diligently.

Once, the tutor noticed the princess' companion was not eating along with her friend. He rebuked her, "Why aren't you eating? Isn't this good enough for you, you ungrateful thing!"

The girl's tears were his answer. She smarted at the insult all day, and that night, at supper, could contain herself no longer. She told the king what the tutor had said. The king reprimanded and even punished him.

Everyone at the palace was fond of the sweet Jewish girl; she had captured their hearts. The older she grew, the more they loved her.

The girls were twelve years old when a fire broke out in the middle of the night. The Jewish girl awoke to the crackling sound of fire and the smell of smoke. She opened up her eyes and saw tongues of flame leaping up the walls of the room. Terrified, she jumped out of the window and began running with all her might, not knowing where she was going. After some time, she reached a wilderness.

"Where are you running?" a voice called out. She stopped and turned to look. There were some shadowy figures nearby.

"What is the rush, little girl?" the voice spoke again. It was a coarse, threatening voice. The Jewish girl had run straight into the arms of a band of ruthless bandits. Seeing that there was no escape and fearing that they might murder her, she suggested, "Why don't you take me to the city and sell me as a servant? You will surely be able to get a large sum for me."

The idea appealed to them. They took her to the nearest city and offered her up for sale.

The news of a Jewish girl being sold at the marketplace reached the ears of the Jewish community. They decided to redeem her and sent off two messengers to the market.

"You can have her for five hundred gold pieces!" the captors demanded. It was an enormous sum of money. Seeing their eyes widen, they added, "If we don't find a buyer at that price, we will kill her."

There was one rich man in the community who agreed to ransom the child. The Shach's daughter was saved.

The congregation saw to all of her needs in the coming years. They provided a home, clothing and an education. When she reached marriageable age she was wedded to the son of her benefactor, the man who had paid her ransom.

Years passed and the community was faced with trouble. A new governor had been appointed over their city. Supplied with the king's permission to deal with its Jewish subjects as he wished, he imposed a heavy tax upon them.

The Jews begged him to reduce the burden. They argued that even if they liquidated all of their assets they would still not be able to pay that huge sum.

But the wicked governor shut his ears to their pleas. "If I do not receive the entire sum by the specified date, you will all suffer!" he threatened.

The Jews gathered in the synagogue and poured out their hearts to the Almighty, begging Him to revoke this impossible decree.

Towards evening, when her husband returned from synagogue, the Shach's daughter noticed his fallen spirits and asked him what troubled him. He told her of the terrible decree issued against the Jews. "Shall I write to the king and ask him to repeal the tax? I know many languages, you know."

"I don't think that anything could help," he murmured. "The new governor is none other than the king's son-in-law.

Do you imagine that the king would honor our word over the governor's?"

"The king's son-in-law?" his wife asked. Hope flared up in her heart. "Then the governor's wife must be the very princess with whom I grew up!" she exclaimed.

"I must see the princess. I must talk to her," she said. "Perhaps I will succeed, with the help of *Hashem*, to nullify the unbearable tax."

She appeared at the governor's mansion the next day, dressed in her best frock. "I am a seamstress," she said to the guards at the gate. "Perhaps the mistress needs the services of an excellent seamstress?"

The governor's wife asked to have the woman shown in. She was impressed by the woman's bearing and began discussing fabrics and styles.

Then, in the midst of the conversation, the 'seamstress' changed the subject and asked, "Do you know who I am?"

"How should I know you? I never saw you before!"

"I am the Jewish girl whom the king took into his palace and raised. I grew up with you. Do you remember the night of the fire? I woke up and panicked. I jumped out of the window and ran far away."

"You are that girl? Really?" the governor's wife asked in amazement, hardly believing her ears. She stood up and approached the young woman and began studying her face. "Indeed you are!" she exclaimed excitedly. "We thought that you had burned to death. How we all grieved for you, especially the king. But here you are, alive and well! Tell me all about yourself and what happened since that fateful night."

The two women sat down and began to reminisce. The Shach's daughter told of her adventures. "And now," she concluded, "I am married and live here in this city." She heaved a deep sigh and fell silent.

"Why are you sighing? You should be happy, being settled

among your people and having a home of your own," said the princess.

"Our community is faced with a grave danger," she confessed. "How shall I not be sorrowful?" The princess looked questioningly and she continued, "A certain official has imposed a very harsh tax upon the Jewish subjects. The sum is so great that if we sold all of our property we could not cover it. Our only hope is to plead with him to be considerate and repeal the tax."

"Who is that official?" the princess asked, but realized at once that it could only be her husband, the governor. "Don't worry!" she reassured her warmly. "The decree will be abolished at once! I promise you!"

Upon his wife's intercession, the governor agreed to revoke the tax.

The Shach's daughter returned home to tell her husband that the mission had succeeded, with the help of the Almighty.

Two years passed. One day a famous rabbi came to the city. He was asked to speak in the synagogue on *Shabbos*. Men and women gathered to hear him, among them the heroine of our story.

As she listened to his speech, she had the eerie feeling of having heard his voice before, but she couldn't place it. "When?" she asked herself. "Who is that man?"

She was very restless throughout the sermon. Something lurked in a corner of her memory. Suddenly, her mind flashed back to the distant past, when she was hardly more than an infant. She heard a singsong voice, a chanting which had filled her days and nights with its background music. She remembered how her father had sat by his huge *gemara*, singing with a voice just like this . . .

Hope sparked in her heart. When she returned home she asked her husband to invite the visitor to their home.

The rabbi agreed. A lively conversation was carried on

during the meal. When the host asked the rabbi about his past, he said, "I once had a little daughter. She was five years old when soldiers invaded our home and made us flee to the forest. But in the midst of my flight she slipped off my back and disappeared. I have searched for her high and low, but she has vanished without a trace ..."

The blood drained from the hostess' face. The rabbi sitting at her table was none other than her father! There could be no mistake about it! She sprang up and shouted, "Father! Father! I am your missing daughter! I am the little girl who was lost in the forest."

The two were reunited. The news spread through the city on wings. The young girl which the community had ransomed from captivity and raised to adulthood was none other than the daughter of the famous Shach, R' Shabsai Hakohen!

"Is it any wonder that she experienced so many wonderful miracles?" people remarked to one another. "She is the daughter of such a great man. Besides, she had the great merit of keeping herself pure. Through all of her trials and adventures, she never ate *treife* food!"

On this day in 5737 (1977), R' Yisrael of Ger passed away. R' Yisrael is called the *Beis Yisrael*, after his work. He was the leader of thousands of Gerrer *chasidim* and myriads of admirers, who flocked to seek his blessing and advice and to hear his words of wisdom. On his *yahrzeit*, thousands visit his grave on the Mt. of Olives in Jerusalem.

The Penetrating Eye of the Rebbe

*E*ach summer the *Beis Yisrael* would spend a few weeks at one of the towns in Israel to relax from his demanding schedule. And each time, the mayor would come to his lodgings to pay his respects.

Once, the mayor said to the *Rebbe*, "The time has come for you to honor me with a return visit. I am a traditional Jew, after all, and deserve that courtesy."

The *Rebbe* surprised the mayor with a question, "Then where are your *tzitzis*?"

The mayor was abashed; he had to admit that he did not wear the required four-fringed garment. He did not again ask the *Rebbe* to visit him . . .

A year passed and an orthodox American Jew visited the town. He met the mayor and they talked together. During the

R' Yisrael Alter, the Beis Yisrael

conversation, the mayor remarked that the Gerrer *Rebbe* was soon due to arrive for his summer vacation.

"I would like to see him!" said the tourist. "I would very much like to visit the Gerrer *Rebbe!*"

"I visit him at his hotel every year," the mayor boasted. "Why don't you join me? I will take you in with me."

Soon after, the *Rebbe* arrived. The mayor and his American guest went to pay their respects.

When they were on the way, the mayor recalled the incident of the previous year about the *tzitzis*. He was suddenly apprehensive that the *Rebbe* might ask if he was wearing *tzitzis*. He turned to his companion and made a strange request, "Would you lend me your *tzitzis* just for this visit?"

The visitor wore his at all times and did not want to remove them now, either, even for a short while. But when the mayor begged and pleaded repeatedly, he felt obliged to consent. They returned to the mayor's office and there, the mayor put on the visitor's *tzitzis*.

They set out again and reached the *Rebbe's* hotel. To their surprise, the *Rebbe* turned to the guest — and not the mayor — and asked, "Where are your *tzitzis*?"

The tourist was dumbfounded. When his wits returned to him, he began hemming and hawing until he finally recounted the whole episode.

The mayor saw clearly, then and there, that one could not escape the *Rebbe's* special sight . . .

3 Adar

On this day in 5372 (1612), R' Mordechai Yaffe passed away. He was born in 5290 (1530) and is considered one of the great *poskim* of our people.

Ten for Ten

R' Mordechai Yaffe's fame spread even among gentile circles and reached the ears of a certain noblewoman. She wanted to marry him and was powerful enough to force him to appear before her.

When he learned of her intentions, he fled from her, passing a sewage pit along the way. He was in such a panic that he jumped into it to get to the other side, soiling all of his clothing, ten garments in all.

At that moment, Heaven granted him the future privilege of writing ten significant works, as reward for the ten soiled garments.

R' Mordechai commemorated that privilege by using the word 'garment' in the title of each of those works: "*Levush Hatecheles, Levush Ateres Zahav, Levush Mordechai*", etc. That is why he is known by the name "The Levush".

4 Adar

On this day in 5067 (1307), the famous R' Meir, the Maharam of Rotenburg, was brought to burial.

Iron Bars Do not Make a Prison

The Maharam of Rotenburg, R' Meir ben R' Baruch, was one of the great *Baalei HaTosafos*. He was born in Worms, Germany, in 4975 (1215) to a family of scholars and leaders. His father, R' Baruch, served as rabbi of Worms and the Maharam often mentioned him with awe.

The following is engraved upon the tombstone of R' Baruch, father of the Maharam: "He sustained the people of his generation with wisdom and good sense; with precious sayings — the fruit of a *tzaddik*, a source of blessing. His fountain spouted for all the isles and cast forth rubies and sapphires."

His brother, R' Avraham, was also a scholar of note.

R' Meir was raised in such a home in which the supporting pillars were Torah and piety. He received the foundation of his knowledge from his father, R' Baruch and later, drank from the wells of other great leaders of his generation, among them, R' Yitzchak of Vienna, author of *Or Zarua* and R' Shmuel of Wurtzburg.

When he was still young, R' Meir traveled to France to study in the *yeshivos* of the *Baalei HaTosafos*: R' Yechiel of Paris, R' Shmuel of Plisse and R' Shmuel of Ivre.

After having filled himself with a wealth of knowledge, he returned to Germany, where he became known as a scholar in his own right, a genius fluent in all the areas and aspects of the Torah. Small wonder that he was soon acknowledged as the leader of German Jewry. Many illustrious communities sought him as their rabbi and he did, in fact, serve in several of them: Kostnitz, Augsburg, Wurtzburg, Rotenburg, Worms, Nurenburg and Mainz.

His longest term of office was in Rotenburg. There, he founded a *yeshivah* which soon became the most vibrant and significant center of Torah throughout Germany.

Students streamed to the *yeshivah* in droves from all the communities of Germany and France. From this *yeshivah* came forth the closest disciples of R' Meir. Thousands of responses to halachic questions of all kinds were sent from there to all the corners of the land.

The Maharam did not only devote himself to the people in his city, but to all the Jews of Germany and France, as a father to his sons. He conducted communal matters with an authoritative hand and fearlessly defended the slightest breach in the fortress of religion. He instituted many regulations and safe-guards to protect Jewry, both spiritually and materially.

Towards the end of his days, the condition of the Jews in Germany deteriorated sadly. Persecution, harsh decrees and riots abounded. The Maharam realized the looming danger and decided to find a haven in a different land.

All of these troubles prompted a wave of emigration from German cities to *Eretz Yisrael*. The Maharam actively promoted the movement and even decided to pull up his roots and go to the Holy Land himself.

The family suffered many hardships until it finally succeeded in leaving the borders of Germany and reaching Lombardi in Italy. The Maharam decided to wait there until additional members of his community joined him, before going up to *Eretz Yisrael*.

While in Lombardi, a convert who recognized him slandered R' Meir before the local authorities. R' Meir was imprisoned and sent back to Germany.

The German emperor, Rudolf, a rabid anti-Semite, ordered R' Meir flung into the dungeon at Anzisheim in Alsace. "He shall be imprisoned here until the Jews pay his ransom," he ruled, setting an exorbitant sum for his release.

All of the communities of Germany labored feverishly to raise the amount needed to free their beloved rabbi.

When the Maharam learned of the huge amount that had been set as a ransom, he forbade the congregations to pay it. He based his ruling upon the words of the *gemara* which say: "Captives must not be ransomed for more than they are worth." This rule was made for the ultimate protection of the Jews, for if evil men saw that the Jews were willing to pay any amount for redeeming their countrymen, they would begin abducting all of our leaders and rabbis to enrich themselves at our expense.

The Jews had no choice but to obey their leader. He re-

mained incarcerated in the Anzisheim dungeon until the end of his days. R' Meir accepted his suffering with loving resign and was a unique example of *kiddush Hashem* for all, Jew and gentile.

The Maharam of Rotenburg was imprisoned for seven years, yet he continued to lead German Jewry as its supreme authority. Despite the fortified stone walls that cloistered him, he continued to teach Torah and even to reply to the many questions that reached him.

Many of his *chiddushim* and his *tosafos* (comments upon the *gemara*) were written in his cell. His disciple, R' Shimshon bar Tzadok, was permitted to visit him frequently. He arranged the work known as *Tashbetz* which the Maharam wrote on Jewish law and custom.

The Maharam kept up an active correspondence with those disciples who were not permitted to visit him. In one such letter written during his stay at Anzisheim, he writes, "I have no access to the works of the *poskim* and if it be found that any of the *tosafos* or other works differ with my opinion in any way, I (automatically) bow to them, for what can the poor man know if he must sit in darkness without any amenities? I have been here already three and a half years, denied all comforts, like a trodden doormat, that creature formerly known as Meir ben R' Baruch . . ."

Surfeited with suffering and sorrow, R' Meir of Rotenburg died in prison on the nineteenth of *Iyar*, 5053 (1293).

But even death did not bring about his release. The German emperor denied him a proper Jewish burial as a punishment for his having preferred to pine away in jail rather than have his brethren pay the ransom which would have filled the royal coffers.

Fourteen years later, the wealthy R' Alexander ben Shlomo Wifman redeemed his remains, at the cost of almost all of his money and property. He asked for only one thing in return, to be buried next to the Maharam when he died.

The Maharam was buried with pomp and ceremony in the Jewish cemetery of Worms on the fourth of *Adar*, 5067 (1307). And when Reb Alexander Wifman passed away, he was buried next to the Maharam.

The Maharam bequeathed to his people a rich spiritual heritage of thousands of responsa which deal with every area of daily life. These served, and still serve, as guides for all of the subsequent *poskim* of succeeding generations to this very day.

Aside from these, he also wrote many *chiddushim* on the Talmud.

The Maharam was also a gifted poet. He composed twenty-four religious *piyutim* (poems) and lamentations in which he describes the beautiful world which *Hashem* created and laments the troubles of our people and degradation of the Torah. His most famous one is *Shaali Serufah Ba'eish* (Ask, O Fire-Seared) which is recited on *Tishah B'Av* along with the other *kinos*.

The Maharam produced many disciples who continued the chain of Torah tradition as rabbis in Jewish communities throughout Germany. Some of the most famous whose teachings are still being studied to this day are: R' Asher ben Yechiel — the Rosh; R' Mordechai ben R' Hillel, author of "Mordechai"; R' Chaim Eliezer ben R' Yitzchak, (author of *Or Zarua*) and R' Yitzchak of Dura.

On this day in 5731 (1971), R' Mordechai Shlomo of Boyan passed away. Shepherd of an illustrious flock of *chasidim* and a 'captain' of orthodox Jewry, his *ahavas Yisrael*, love for his fellow Jew, was unique. R' Mordechai Shlomo was born on the thirteenth of *Tishrei* in 5651 (1891) and passed away in the United States. He is buried on the Mt. of Olives in Jerusalem and his grave has become a holy shrine for many Jews in distress.

Do Not Disturb

*I*t was the eve of *Lag B'Omer*. Multitudes of young and old, men, women and children, streamed to the northern part of *Eretz Yisrael*, to Mount Meron where the saintly *tana*, Rabban Shimon bar Yochai, is buried.

Among the many pilgrims was the *Rebbe* of Boyan, who also wished to pour out his prayers at the holy site.

R' Mordechai bore a special love for the place. When he visited *Eretz Yisrael*, he would lead a large congregation of his followers to Mount Meron. There, he would be honored with the lighting of the huge bonfire upon the roof of the Rashbi's cave. This privilege had become a permanent honor handed down to him from his holy forefathers, dating back to R' Yisrael of Ruzhin.

It was a sweltering evening and the tongues of red

R' Mordechai Shlomo of Boyan

flames leaping up from the immense bonfire intensified the heat.

The following day the Boyaner *Rebbe* participated joyfully in the celebrations which took place — the *chalakah* — the haircuts performed on three-year-old boys which dates back to the days of the Ari. He was honored with the first snip, as hundreds of little Jewish boys were shorn of their locks. Upon the conclusion of this ceremony, he entered the tomb and, again, poured out his heart in fervent prayer.

One group of *chasidim* tried to clear a path through the congested myriads of visitors. They pushed their way up to the entrance of the cave to enable the *Rebbe* to pass. For they knew how much it meant to him. But the *Rebbe* had his own thoughts on the matter.

"Stay where you are!" he said to the *chasidim*. Hundreds of his followers stood still, like soldiers obeying orders.

"I do not want to enter. I am happy where I am. I wish to pray together with my fellow Jews. Far be it from me to disturb Jews at their prayers!"

The *chasidim* remained where they were, waiting for their turn to approach the cave.

A whisper passed among the people: "The Boyaner *Rebbe* is near the entrance, but cannot proceed." At that moment, people from within the cave began flowing out. "Make way! Make way!" they cried as they slowly progressed.

Behold the wonder: Within a few moments a path had been cleared for the *tzaddik*, as if a highway had been laid in a sea of humanity.

The *Rebbe*, gripped in his holy thoughts, did not even notice the unusual movement erupting all around him. When his *chasidim* turned to him and said, "*Rebbe*, the way ahead is clear. You can enter now," he looked up from his *siddur* and glanced all around him in surprise; a look of dissatisfaction crossed his face.

"Is all this commotion because of me?" he asked bitterly. "Have Jews left the holy site in the middle of their prayers because of me?

"I would just as soon pray here rather than disturb a Jew in the midst of his prayers, G-d forbid!" He shifted his gaze back to his *siddur* and continued saying *Tehillim* with great concentration.

Respect for Others

Upon one of his visits to *Eretz Yisrael*, R' Mordechai Shlomo brought along a precious heirloom which had been handed down from his holy forefathers.

It was a coin which he cherished dearly and guarded carefully. He would take it wherever he went, so as best to keep his eye on it at all times.

Once, during the *Rebbe's* stay, his hotelkeeper was cleaning, when he happened to notice a large, unusual coin in the corner of a room. As he stooped to pick it up, he remembered that the *Rebbe* always carried around an unusual coin. This must be it! How distressed the *Rebbe* must be, for surely he had already discovered that it was gone. The hotelkeeper, a *chasid*, decided to locate the *Rebbe* immediately and return the coin to him.

He set the broom aside, put on his jacket and ran swiftly to the *Rebbe's* room. He knocked on the door and waited for it to be opened. When he was admitted, he walked directly up to the *Rebbe* and held out the coin.

The *Rebbe's* eyes lit up and he became very excited.

"May you be blessed! What a kindness you just performed in returning lost property! I have been looking for that very coin for several days, but in vain. I was heartbroken. But now that you have found it, may you and your family be forever blessed for having made me so happy!"

The *Rebbe* heaped blessing upon blessing on the bewildered *chasid's* head.

"But, *Rebbe*," the hotelkeeper said, "why didn't you tell me that you had lost it, in the first place? I am familiar with this hotel; I know every corner in it. I would have helped you look for it!"

"Yes, I am aware of that. You would have been of great help. But," the *Rebbe* lowered his voice and said, "there is a poor maid who is employed here. I was afraid that suspicion might have fallen upon her.

"I, therefore, decided to contain my sorrow rather than seek help in my search."

He continued, "The coin is very dear and precious to me, but the pride and self-respect of that poor maid is seven times dearer!"

A Stench of Heresy

The Boyaner *Rebbe* was a veritable encyclopedia of fine character traits. He never hurt or insulted another in the least, but went out of his way to show his respect for humanity.

Nevertheless, it once happened — and only once — that someone had to flee from him.

R' Meshulam Zusha Portugal, the Skulener *Rebbe*, who was bound heart and soul to the Boyaner *Rebbe*, was present at that unusual event and told the story. The *Admorim* of the Ruzhiner dynasty had a custom of praying in a room adjacent to the *beis medrash*. The Boyaner *Rebbe* never interfered in any way with internal matters of the *beis knesses*. His prayer was all heart and mind; it was like the fire smoldering upon the *mizbe'ach*.

Once, a distinguished-looking stranger entered the *beis medrash* in Vienna, turned to the *gabbaim* and humbly asked if he could lead the prayers that day since he had an 'obligation', a *yahrzeit*.

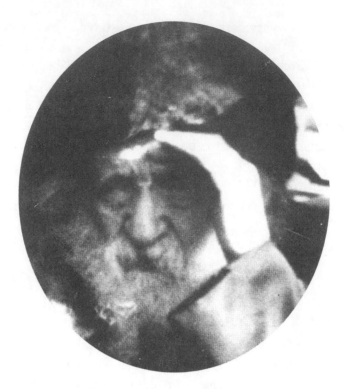

R' Meshulam Zusha Portugal, the Skulener Rebbe

They agreed; such things were commonplace. But as soon as the stranger began leading the prayer, the Boyaner *Rebbe* emerged from his room, walked up to the *chazzan* and asked why he was there.

"I have a *chiyuv* today (obligation)," he explained.

"Perhaps you are under obligation to lead the prayers, but who says that I am under obligation to hear you?" the *Rebbe* said, his eyes burning. The *chasidim* had never seen him like this.

As soon as the *Rebbe* had uttered his brief remark, the stranger removed his *tallis* and *tefillin*, left them on the *amud* (prayer stand) and ran out of the synagogue.

Several curious *chasidim* wished to understand what had just taken place. They inquired and learned that the stranger, who had appeared to be so respectable, was really a famous scoundrel and apostate. He had wagered a large sum that he could fool even a great *Rebbe*. He claimed that the *Rebbes* were unaware of what was happening about them.

The heretic not only lost a considerable sum of money, but became a laughingstock among his friends.

Had not the prophet Yeshayahu said that *tzaddikim* were blessed with a sense of 'smelling out', so to speak, "And he shall smell out the fear of G-d" (11:3)? From his isolated room, without even seeing the man's face, he was able to sense that he was an impostor. His finely tuned perception made him aware of that man's true nature.

I Am with Him in Sorrow

*I*t was 5727 (1967). War was in the air in *Eretz Yisrael*. The Arabs were poised threateningly on all the borders of the land, ready to wipe the little country off the face of the earth.

One evening, a group of Torah leaders held a meeting in America to decide what could be done about the dangerous situation in the Holy Land. The rabbis were in the midst of a heated discussion when the door opened and R' Mordechai Shlomo of Boyan entered.

His appearance caused a great stir among those present, since everyone knew that he had been bedridden with a critical illness and forbidden to leave his room.

The doctors' orders were one thing and the *Rebbe's* will — another. The *Rebbe* would not dream of missing such an important meeting. The rabbis had considered holding it in his house to enable him to participate. But the doctors had vehemently opposed this suggestion, as well.

"On no account!" they said emphatically. "To do so would be endangering the *Rebbe's* life. He must have absolute quiet and peace of mind; by no means must he become agitated for it would have a drastic effect upon his health."

The rabbis had been resigned to the *Rebbe's* absence. But the *Rebbe* thought otherwise. Let the doctors say what they would — if his people were in danger and needed Heavenly mercy, how could he remain home?

He left his sickbed with superhuman effort, dressed himself in warm clothing and dragged himself to the meeting — even though he had not ventured beyond his bedroom for the longest time.

The rabbis at the gathering were shocked to see the panting *Rebbe* framed in the doorway, looking weak and pale.

When they voiced their concern about his health, he apologized and said, "To be honest, it was quite difficult for me to come. But it was still more difficult to remain at home! I could not stand by at this time of great need. Please, let me do what my heart tells me."

The rabbis understood that it was indeed better for the *Rebbe* to be here with them, sharing their anxiety, than to remain at home alone, anxious and distressed.

The discussion went on for many hours, throughout which the *Rebbe* sat, visibly suffering excruciating pain. From time to time he would give a shudder and try to overcome some sharp pang. He would shut his eyes tightly for a moment, pull himself together and then rejoin the discussion, as if nothing had occurred.

By the end of the exhausting conference, the *Rebbe* was drained and on the verge of collapse. His bouts of pain increased and became more frequent. And when he tried to rise from his seat, he let out a heavy sigh which revealed the severity of his condition.

The rabbis were instantly at his side, trying to help him. But instead of replying to their anxious questions, he gave another sigh, deeper than the first one, and began to shake.

The rabbis saw how the exertion of the meeting had affected him. But they did not know what to do to ease his pain, which became more and more acute.

In the voiced undercurrent of concern, there was a whisper. "Was it really so important for the *Rebbe* to come, if it meant actually risking his life?"

The whisper reached the pain-racked *Rebbe*. His eyes shot sparks and his voice grew stronger as he replied, "And what's so wrong? When Jewish lives are in danger, I can also bow my back to share their suffering." With these words, he suddenly felt relieved and revived. His body straightened and he rose from his chair. Now he was able to make his way back home, accompanied by the entire gathering of awed admirers.

On the evening of this day, on the eve of the seventh of *Adar* II in 5581 (1821), R' Yitzchak Isaac Taub passed away. R' Yitzchak Isaac was a sublimely holy man and the founder of the Kaliv dynasty of chasidic leaders.

The Fire is Doused

R' Yitzchak Isaac Taub of Kaliv once spent a *Shabbos* in a village not far from his town. During *kabbolas Shabbos* the cry went up that the silos of his host were afire. All the grain would go up in smoke, a devastating loss for the farmer. When R' Yitzchak Isaac saw that the Jew was about to leave the synagogue to go and save his property, he grasped him by the arm and said, "Stop! Wait! Let me tell you a true story:

"R' Zusha of Anipoli used to say *Tehillim* by the stove in the *beis medrash* of his master, the *Maggid* of Mezeritch, as the *Shabbos* was being ushered in. Once, as he was deeply immersed in psalms, people began shouting, 'Fire!' Fire had, indeed, broken out from the intense heat of the stove. R' Zusha, sitting right beside it, was oblivious to the danger. 'Zusha, fire!' they cried in alarm. But he continued on with his psalms. When they yelled 'Fire!' once more, he replied, 'And so what if there is a fire? Does the Torah not say, 'And the fire subsided?' At these words the fire did, in fact, subside.

"And that is what I say now," concluded the *Rebbe* of Kaliv reassuringly. "It says in the Torah, 'And the fire subsided'."

Thereupon, this fire, also, died down and went out. Later, when they went to assess the damage, they discovered a deep recess within the granary, into which the fire had sunk and burnt itself out.

7 Adar

On this day in 2488, Moshe *Rabbenu* passed away.

Moshe and Yehoshua

Thus did *Hashem* say to Moshe, "Ascend Mount Avarim and gaze upon the land which I am giving to the Israelites. Then die as Aharon your brother died."

Moshe could already imagine the Jews walking through the desert like a flock without a shepherd, and, weepingly, he said to *Hashem*, "You know the thoughts of man. Appoint a merciful, forbearing and compassionate leader for the Jews, a humble man who will be able to bear the vexations of the people and their quarrels. Make him patient towards them and their children. Let him lead them in war and not, as do other kings, remain safe in the comforts of his castle and send his servants to fight against the enemy."

Hashem heard Moshe's request and said, "You asked for a successor. I will show you all of the judges and prophets who will serve the people from now until *techiyas hameisim*."

He first showed him Yehoshua, then Osniel ben Kenaz and the judges and prophets of each generation down through the ages. And He said, "All these are of one mind and one spirit. I will show you one with a special spirit; Him, you will see last, for he is the *mashiach* who will come in the end of days. His spirit will weigh down those of all the prophets and leaders who have come before him.

"And now, take Yehoshua, who served you all these years, for he will succeed you. He will lead the Jews out of the desert and bring them to the Land of Canaan. You thought that your sons would take your place, but Yehoshua, who served you so faithfully and respected you so greatly, is best fit for that task. Yehoshua is a man after your own heart, as you have surely seen countless times. He shall lead the people, each and every one. Go, Moshe, and place your hand upon his head. Appoint him to ask, seek, instruct and command in your lifetime so that when you depart from this world, the Jews will not say, 'He never had any authority in Moshe's lifetime. Shall he have it now that Moshe is gone?'"

Moshe went to Yehoshua and told him what *Hashem* had said. Yehoshua burst into tears and said, "My master, your words are difficult to accept."

Moshe replied, "Rise and be strong, Yehoshua. Become the head of the people!"

Yehoshua had no desire for this at all. He wanted to pray to *Hashem* to extend Moshe's life so that he could lead the Jews into the Holy Land. But Moshe stopped him, saying, "*Hashem* is not like mortals who regret what they have once said. If He swore that I would not enter the Land, He will surely fulfill His word."

Yehoshua said, "Who am I to come in your stead and take your place? I am not suited for the task at all!"

Yehoshua refused to lead the people. Moshe tried, at length, to convince him to accept authority and said, "From the

day that I knew you, Yehoshua, I saw that you love kindness and charity. Let me, then, tell you this: Lead the
people faithfully with all your heart. This will be the greatest
act of kindness and charity that you will have done until this
day."

These words convinced Yehoshua. For he did indeed desire
to pursue good acts and kindness.

When Moshe saw that Yehoshua was willing, he said to
him, "I will now place my hands upon your head to fortify
you. My strength will flow to you, so that the people will
respect you when you lead them. I also have some advice to
give you for your own good."

"Whatsoever you tell me — I shall most certainly do!"
replied Yehoshua.

Moshe said, "Know that the Jews are, still, like a young boy
who does not yet know that he must choose what is good and
despise what is evil. Therefore, if they provoke you, do not be
angry with them. If they sin against you, do not punish them.
Instead, increase your love towards them and remember that
they also angered *Hashem* — Who holds all living things in
His hand — countless times. Yet He did not destroy them. If
you promise me that you will always be merciful towards
them, like a father to his children, you will set my mind at ease
and sweeten the last days of my life."

Yehoshua burst into tears and promised Moshe to do as he
had said. Moshe then laid his hands upon Yehoshua's head
and he became filled to overflowing with the spirit of wisdom
and intelligence, wise council and courage. Moshe also gave of
his radiance so that the face of Yehoshua shone like that of
Moshe himself. For rays of light emanated from Moshe's
countenance, like the rays which emanate from the sun.

Our Sages said that at that moment, Moshe resembled a
flaming torch which had lit many candles but whose light had
not been diminished. As the saying goes: A light for one is a

light for a hundred. Thus, Moshe transmitted his wisdom and prophecy to Yehoshua. His grandeur and glory, along with his wisdom and prophecy, still remained intact.

Moshe convinced Yehoshua with words — good words, appeasing words — and informed him that a great reward awaited him and all other Jewish leaders in the World-to-Come.

Moshe brought Yehoshua before Elazar Hakohen and before the entire people and installed him as the new leader, his successor. He made a momentous occasion out of it, because he wanted the Jews to respect and fear Yehoshua.

Moshe lifted Yehoshua off the ground and sat him on the seat near him. All the people raised their heads and bent their ears to hear Yehoshua's words. He said: "Blessed is *Hashem*, Who gave His Torah to the people of Israel through Moshe *Rabbenu*."

Moshe showed great respect towards Yehoshua. Whenever Yehoshua would enter the place of study, Moshe would hush the translator and tell him to wait until Yehoshua would be seated. Whenever Israel encamped, Moshe's criers would pass through among the people and announce that Yehoshua "is worthy of being the G-d-designated shepherd."

When Moshe and Yehoshua stood before the people, Moshe said, "See these people, Yehoshua? They are being entrusted into your care. There are infants among them who have never performed any *mitzvos*. Heed yourself, lest you say something improper for they are the sons of the Almighty. *Hashem* refers to them as 'My firstborn, Yisrael.' He favors them above all other peoples and tongues."

"What shall I do if, in apportioning the land, I give one a mountainous plot when he wants one in the plain?"

"Fear not!" Moshe reassured him. "*Hashem* promised me that the division of the land would be carried out peaceably."

Moshe then beckoned to Yehoshua to draw close. He kissed

him and wept upon his neck. "I bless you that you should live in peace with the people." Moshe said this after he had chastised, scolded and reproved the people throughout his days.

And This is the Blessing

Before his death, Moshe compared the Torah to dew and its commandments to rain.

He was asked why he had done so.

Moshe replied, "Just as dew and rain make the grass grow and the trees blossom anew, so does the Torah heal all flesh and invigorate the bones. It is a source of life to all who grasp it. Therefore, my brothers, heed the Torah and observe its commandments with all your heart and soul. If you do so, *Hashem* will love you, multiply you and bless you throughout the land."

Moshe then turned to bless each tribe. But, before he did so, he said, "I have burdened you with the Torah and its commandments. Please forgive me."

They replied, "Our master, you are forgiven. We, too, angered you and bothered you exceedingly. Forgive us!"

Moshe replied, "You are forgiven."

Moshe first blessed Reuven. He said: "Long live Reuven! May his descendants be mighty in battle and great in Torah!"

He blessed Shimon and Yehudah thus: "May *Hashem* answer you in your time of need — when you call upon Him, may He draw near! And when you cry unto Him, may He hear you."

He blessed Levi thus: "You *Leviim*, who were steadfast and did not bow before the Golden Calf, who punished the idolatrous, even when they were relatives, your reward will be to teach the people the laws of *Hashem*."

To Binyamin he said, "Fortunate are you, Binyamin, a friend of *Hashem*, for the *Beis Hamikdash* will be built in your portion and *Hashem* will reside there forever."

When the rest of the tribes heard his words to Binyamin, they said, "Why is Binyamin so privileged to be called the 'friend of *Hashem*' and why has he been given all that is holy to us?"

Moshe replied, "Don't you know that Binyamin is different? You were born in an impure land while he was born in *Eretz Yisrael*. You were all present when Yosef was sold as a slave, while Binyamin was at home. *Hashem* will not build His House in the portion of people who showed no compassion for a brother and sold him into slavery. Besides, when Yaakov grew old and could no longer come and go as before, Binyamin attended him. While all of you were concerned about your families and your welfare, he sat by his father's side, obeyed his wishes, fed him, gave him to drink and did everything for him. *Hashem*, therefore, said, 'Because Yaakov leaned on Binyamin's shoulders, I will raise him up and exalt him. And I, too, shall dwell between his shoulders'."

Moshe said to Yosef, "You fulfilled the will of your Creator, therefore your portion will be the most blessed. It will lack nothing. Heavenly dew will water your streams and fountains will gush from your valleys and mountains. Your entire land will abound in water and will be a veritable garden of *Hashem*."

Zevulun was blessed as follows: "You shall trade with all lands and will become wealthy. You shall support your brother Yissachar and enable him to study Torah night and day and increase his wisdom. All of his sons shall be scholars."

"The fruit of your land shall be sweet to everyone's palate," said Moshe to Naftali. "Your land will be blessed and its inhabitants content."

To Asher he said, "You, Asher, will produce fine oil which will be in great demand. People will come from afar to buy your oil and will pay for it with fields and vineyards. You will be a favorite of your brothers."

Thus did Moshe bless all of the tribes. And when he ended, he turned to the entire nation, spread his palms Heavenward, and prayed, "Please, *Hashem*, save Your people and bless Your heritage, guide them and raise them forever more."

8 Adar

This is the day following the death of Moshe.

Tzaddikim Live on Even in Death

H adrian, the Roman emperor, once boasted to R' Yehoshua ben Chananya, "I am greater than Moshe."

"Why do you say so?" R' Yehoshua asked.

"Because I am alive and he is dead. In *Koheles* it says, 'For a live dog is better than a dead lion' (9:4).

"If that is so," replied R' Yehoshua, "then issue a proclamation forbidding any Roman to light a fire for three days."

The emperor agreed. A proclamation was made. No one was to light a fire for three days.

Night fell. Hadrian and R' Yehoshua went up to the roof of the palace. They looked all about them and noticed pillars of smoke rising in the distance. Where there is smoke there is fire. The emperor sent a servant to investigate. It was discovered that several people, throughout the city, had defied Hadrian's decree and lit fires under some pretext or another.

R' Yehoshua then turned to the emperor and said, "You are a living monarch ruling over your land, yet you are not powerful enough to enforce your decree for even one night! Moshe our teacher is dead over one thousand years. Nevertheless, he taught us the commandment that we must not light fires throughout our dwellings on the Sabbath day. Have you ever seen a Jew lighting a fire on *Shabbos*? Now, do you still claim that you are greater than Moshe ..." (According to *Yalkut Shimoni, Koheles, 989*)

On this day, in 5548 (1788), R' Shlomo Zalman of Volozhin passed away. R' Shlomo Zalman was the brother of the renowned R' Chaim of Volozhin. He was born on the 26th of *Sivan*, 5516 (1756), and was one of the elect disciples of the *Gaon* of Vilna. He was a brilliant scholar and a sublime *tzaddik*.

Doctor's Orders

R' Shlomo Zalman of Volozhin, or R' Zalmele, as people referred to him, was a great scholar. His greatness was not only expressed through his vast knowledge, but mainly by his noble character. His modesty and humility were his most outstanding traits. Small wonder that people said that throughout his life he fulfilled the teaching of R' Chanina ben Dosa, "If a person is favored by his fellow man, he is also favored by the Almighty." And indeed, people loved R' Zalmele for his genuinely warm personality, and he was beloved by Heaven for that very quality.

R' Zalmele and his attendant once happened to visit the home of a Vilna Jew. It was afternoon and the family was seated at the table.

When the famous visitor entered the house, he was greeted warmly by the master. "Please, won't you do us the great honor of joining us for dinner?" he begged.

R' Zalmele politely declined. He knew that the host was a poor man who struggled to put food on his table. Besides, a hasty glance at the table already told him that this was a meal which would hardly suffice for the family.

The host pleaded again and again, but each time R' Zalmele politely refused. Finally, when he feared that the master of the house might become insulted by his many refusals, he apologized, "The truth is that I could not join you, since my doctor forbids me to eat such food."

The host finally accepted this excuse. Who was he to argue with a doctor's orders? R' Zalmele's attendant, however, raised his eyebrows questioningly. He had never known that R' Zalmele was suffering from any illness. Could it be that a *tzaddik* as great as R' Zalmele would utter a lie?

It seems that the incredulous expression remained on his face throughout the visit. On their way back, R' Zalmele turned to him and explained, "As you know, the Rambam was a famous doctor. He ruled that a man must not be a guest at a meal which is not sufficient for the hosts, for this is comparable to theft."

On the evening following this day, on the eve of the eleventh of *Adar*, R' Chaim Yosef David Azulai passed away. The Chida, as he was called, was brilliant in the revealed and the mystic areas of the Torah. Saintly in every aspect, he authored over one hundred works on Torah subjects. He was born in *Sivan*, 5484 (1724), and died in 5566 (1806) during a stay in Livorno, Italy. One hundred and fifty-four years later, in 5720 (1960), his remains were brought to Jerusalem and buried on *Har Hamenuchos*. His grave has become a prayer site for multitudes who come to seek Heavenly assistance.

The Lines Which Bore Witness to the Writer

During one of the Chida's visits in Germany, he went to the city of Worms to make the acquaintance of a famous Jewish leader, R' Yaakov Yehoshua Pollak, author of *Pnei Yehoshua*.

The *Pnei Yehoshua* welcomed his visitor from *Eretz Yisrael* as he did everyone who crossed his threshold, especially one from the Holy Land. He invited him to be his guest without realizing his uniqueness and holiness.

During the days that the Chida remained under his roof, he

R' Chaim Yosef David Azulai

attended all of R' Yaakov Yehoshua's *shiurim*, but out of modesty, did not enter into the scholarly discussions, even though he could have contributed.

The Chida left Worms after two weeks, for the next stop of his extended journey throughout Europe to disseminate Torah and raise money for the settlements in the Holy Land. Before leaving, he went to pay his respects to his kind host, who was taken by this impressive Jew and gave him his new *sefer*, the second volume of *Pnei Yehoshua*, as a gift.

On the following day, when R' Yaakov Yehoshua was sitting before the scholars who attended his daily lecture, the door shot open and Yitzchak Lipman the peddler burst in. He was a worthy Jew who was always in a hurry. Puffing and panting, sweat dripping from his brow, he held a large sack in one hand and his *tallis* and *tefillin* bag in the other.

Breathlessly, he said, "I was returning home from prayers this morning, in a rush to reach home, when I almost tripped over a sack. I bent down to see what it was and saw that it contained *sefarim* and notebooks full of scholarly material. 'These must belong to some learned man,' I guessed, and thought to bring them here. The rabbi can decide what to do with them."

The door slammed shut. Yitzchak Lipman was already on his way, speeding on, as usual.

The *Pnei Yehoshua* inspected the contents of the sack after he had finished that day's lecture.

Together with the participants of the *shiur* he examined the writings for a clue as to their owner.

The sack was so stuffed that they had to remove the contents with utmost care so as not to tear anything. This was someone else's property, after all.

Suddenly, one of the students exclaimed, "Look! Here is our master's *sefer*, the one that just came off the press the other day. And see! The margins are already filled with notations."

Everyone gathered around to read the comments written in a fluent style which testified to the scholarship of its writer.

"He must be a real genius!" they exclaimed in unison. "Look how perceptive his remarks are. His comments indicate an encyclopedic grasp of the entire *Shas* and *poskim*!"

The rabbi now took the volume into his hands and recognized it as the copy he had given to the Chida.

"I know who that brilliant scholar is!" he announced. "It is the wonderful guest who departed from my house just yesterday and who attended this *shiur* during his stay. He probably did not join in the discussion out of great modesty."

The rabbi continued to study the notes, his amazement growing from moment to moment.

"I gave him this book only yesterday and he has already completed studying it and writing incisive comments upon it! There is truly no Torah like the Torah of *Eretz Yisrael!"*

"Alas, a man of G-d was in this place and I did not know it!" he said with a sigh and sent his *shammash* to overtake the Chida and return his lost property to him.

Before the messenger left, he said, "Ask him to mention me in his prayers and ask him to forgive me for not having accorded him the proper respect."

The Chida never forgot his meeting with the famous *Pnei Yehoshua*. He writes about him as follows in his biographical work *Shem Hagedolim*:

> His fame spread throughout the world thanks to his pure work, the *Pnei Yehoshua*, a four-volume commentary on the Talmud. And I, as a young man, had the privilege of 'greeting the *Shechinah*', so to speak, and basking in his presence for several days. His appearance is that of a Heavenly angel. He gave me the gift of his second volume of *Pnei Yehoshua* on *Moed*, which had just been published.

An Empty Vessel

The Chida was not known only for his brilliance and holiness but also for a wisdom and intelligence which won him fame among Jews and gentiles alike.

A boorish man once came to the Chida for a letter of recommendation addressed to the rabbi of a different city, attesting to his honesty and reliability. He insisted that the letter lavish praise on him. The Chida was reluctant to do so but the man pressed and even threatened him. Since there was no one in the *beis midrash*, at the time, to come to his aid, he had no alternative but to write the requested letter.

But in his wisdom, he found a way to indicate to the rabbi not to take his letter seriously.

He wrote in such glowing terms that even the man, himself, marveled at it. He capped the letter with, "This man is so great that had he lived in the times of the prophet Elisha, the oil would never have stopped flowing." (In *Melachim II, Chapter 4* we are told of the poor widow whose husband had been a prophet. Elisha told her to gather empty vessels and pour the remainder of the little oil she still possessed into these vessels. The widow's flask of oil was blessed and she kept pouring from it until she had filled all of the vessels which she had gathered.)

The man exulted in his victory. He had succeeded in intimidating the great rabbi and gained a letter full of flowery praise.

The rabbi in the distant city read the long letter of recommendation. He sensed that such a great man as the Chida must be hinting at something between the lines. He finally understood: The Chida was telling him that the man was no more than an 'empty vessel', a man without content, and that the letter had been extorted under pressure.

Needless to say, the man received his just deserts there; he was chased out of town in disgrace.

The evening following this day, the twelfth of *Adar*, is mentioned in *Megillas Taanis*. On this day, *Hashem*'s name was sanctified through the act of two worthy brothers, Pappus and Lulianus. These two sacrificed their lives to save their brethren. Later, this day was designated as one of joy, on which fasting or eulogizing the dead was forbidden. With the passing of time, however, it was no longer viewed as a joyous one, since on that day two other worthy brothers, Shemayah and Achiyah, were also killed.

Two Brothers

*T*rajan was one of the most infamous of Roman emperors. He persecuted the Jews with a vengeance.

One day the emperor's daughter was found dead in the city of Lod. No one knew who had killed her. "I have no enemies in this city who might have wanted to kill her," Trajan said, "except the Jews. They must be her murderers."

In his wrath, he decreed death to all the Jews of Lod.

There were two brothers living in Lod at the time, the righteous Pappus and Lulianus. Fearing for the fate of their brethren, they came before the emperor and confessed, "We killed the princess. We are the guilty ones."

Trajan could tell that they were lying; all they wanted to do was protect their fellow Jews. Nevertheless, he accepted their confession. He could not do otherwise, since they even suggested a motive for killing her.

The two were sentenced to die. When they were led to the execution, the emperor said to them, "If you belong to the people of Chananyah, Mishael and Azaryah, then your G-d will surely rescue you from my hands, as he rescued them from Nebuchadnezzar."

They replied, "Chananyah, Mishael and Azaryah were perfect *tzaddikim* and worthy of a miracle. Besides, Nebuchadnezzar was a decent king and worthy of being involved in a miracle. But you are not a worthy cause for effecting a miracle, nor are we, for we already deserve to die. If you don't kill us, then Heaven will find another messenger to carry out Its will. There are lions and bears who can kill us. But Heaven chose to have us die by your hand so that G-d can later demand vengeance for our blood and punish you."

The emperor heard, but did not change his mind. He had them killed.

It is told that after their death and before their burial, two men arrived at the place of execution. They appeared to be important officials. They assassinated Trajan viciously, battering his head open with logs which they found strewn about. Thus, the prophecy of the two brothers came true: Heaven had permitted the emperor to kill them, so as to have an excuse to avenge their blood upon him.

That day was the 11th of *Adar*. Our Sages designated it as a day on which a miracle occurred and called it 'The Day of Turianus (Trajan).'

The two holy brothers, Pappus and Lulianus, are mentioned in many places as the Martyrs of Lod. They are so sanctified that it is said that no one can stand in their presence in *Gan Eden*.

But the joy of the eleventh of *Adar* was stilled by the death of two other worthy brothers, Shemayah and Achiyah, who were killed on this very day, many years later. The reason is unknown.

12 Adar

On the evening of this day, on the thirteenth of *Adar*, in 5746 (1986), R' Moshe Feinstein passed away. Born on the 7th of *Adar* in 5655 (1895), he was known as the ultimate halachic authority of the generation and a truly pious man.

Denouncing Pride

From early childhood, people prophesied a brilliant future for the young Moshe Feinstein. His father, the brilliant R' David, invested all of his might and soul to bring him up with fine character traits and have him gain vast knowledge of Torah.

Once when Moshe was eleven, he entered the room where his father was sitting together with other rabbis. The moment he entered, all the rabbis stood up on their feet, for, even then, he had gained the reputation of brilliance and they felt they must honor him.

R' David, the boy's father, reacted strongly. "What are you doing to me?" he cried. "You are destroying my son! You will fill him with arrogance!"

R' Moshe Feinstein

The boy heard his father's strong words decrying pride and was deeply impressed. Many years later he would recall that incident and note how deeply it was etched in his memory.

After Yom Kippur

A Jew once came to R' Moshe Feinstein asking for a letter of recommendation. The rabbi wrote one without hesitation.

Later, when he had gone, the people in the room expressed their surprise. "How," they asked, "could *Rabbenu* help that man when it is known that he attacked you in public not long ago?"

R' Moshe replied, "*Yom Kippur* has already passed since then and I, like all Jews, forgave anyone who insulted me. Did you expect me to bear a grudge against a person whom I already forgave with all my heart?"

The Mitzvah-Messenger

T he winter of 5721 (1961) was a harsh one in America. Snow fell constantly, confining millions of people to their homes. The subways and trains were shut down; the entire state of New York and much of the country was paralyzed.

New York City suffered greatly. Snow had fallen and piled up for over a week and it was freezing, sub-zero weather. The streets were deserted. In R' Moshe's house, he and his family were having a heated discussion.

The great man had been invited to the wedding of a relative that evening. He was determined to go.

"Do you think that the *mitzvah* of gladdening the hearts of the *chasan* and *kallah* is one to be taken lightly?" he demanded. "*Hashem* Himself did so for Adam and Chavah (*Bereishis Rabbah 8*); so did the *tannaim* and *amoraim* (*Avos d'R' Nasan 41*)."

But his family was concerned about the rabbi's health, for he was no longer young. They tried to dissuade him from going. "In such weather, no one else will be going, either," they argued.

That very argument decided the issue.

"Well, if no one else will attend, then I, surely, am obliged to go!" he declared.

He left his house and went to the wedding. And he returned safely, as it says, "Messengers performing a *mitzvah* are not harmed" (*Pesachim 8*).

Taanis Esther. On this day Mordechai and Esther assembled all the Jews in Shushan for a day of fasting and prayer to entreat Heaven that they be victorious in the battle for their lives which would take place the following day, on the fourteenth of *Adar*. This was not the first fast. Almost a year before, on *Pesach* eve, they fasted for three days and nights to ask *Hashem* to revoke Haman's decree. Even the little children participated in this fast.

The Children's Cry

After Haman prepared the gallows for Mordechai, he went to look for him. He found him in the *beis midrash*, sitting before twenty-two thousand Jewish children, all wrapped in sackcloth, tearfully studying Torah.

Haman encircled the place with iron chains and set guards to watch them. He said, "Tomorrow I will kill these children. Then I will hang Mordechai."

The children's mothers came to bring them bread and water. They said, "Dear sons! Eat and drink before you die. You need not die hungry."

But the twenty-two thousand children laid their hands upon their books and swore: "Upon the life of our master Mordechai, we shall not eat or drink. Let them kill us in our fast." The children then burst into heavy weeping which rose all the way to Heaven.

Hashem's compassion was aroused and He moved from His throne of justice to the throne of mercy. Then He took the letters containing Haman's evil decrees — and tore them to shreds!

Purim. A day of special prayers, feasting, sending gifts to friends and giving money to the poor to commemorate the saving of the Jews in Shushan, Persia.

The Only Counsel

When Haman decided to destroy and annihilate all of the Jews, he first gathered together all of his advisers to discuss the most efficient plan of action.

Haman had a friend called Zaharan. When Haman told him what he sought to do to the Jews and told him about the lots he had drawn, Zaharan said, "You resemble the foolish heron which decided to dry up the ocean."

"What do you mean?"

Zaharan explained: "A heron once built its nest by the seashore. Once, it left its fledglings in the nest and went to forage for food. When it returned it saw that the nest had

disappeared. The waves had washed it away, destroying it and drowning the little herons.

"The heron was so enraged at the sea that it threatened revenge. It would transfer all of the waters of the sea to the shore, thus turning the sea into dry land.

"It began, carrying water in its beak and pouring it upon the shore. It did this repeatedly until it was exhausted. By nightfall, the heron felt that its strength was failing. Nevertheless, driven by anger, it continued to work, fetching water from the sea and pouring it on the shore.

"Along came another bird and watched the heron's frantic activity. Finally, it asked, 'What in the world are you doing?'

"The heron explained what the sea had done to its nest and fledglings. 'I have vowed to take revenge,' it declared, 'and will not stop, until I transform the sea to dry land!'

"The little bird burst into laughter and said, 'Even if you were to work for the rest of your life, from morning to evening, you would never succeed, you foolish bird!'"

Zaharan hoped that Haman would see the parallel but Haman said, "Your story does not apply to this situation. If King Achashverosh empowers me to destroy the Jews, I will certainly succeed. Besides, I happen to know that the G-d of the Jews has abandoned them, for they sinned doubly against Him. They bowed down to the idol in *Bavel* and compounded their sin here in Shushan by partaking of King Achashverosh's feast against the orders of their leader, Mordechai, my sworn enemy."

The advisers continued to discuss the matter but no one gave him better advice than his wife Zeresh.

"If this Mordechai is of Jewish descent," she said, "then you will never succeed in destroying him and his people through a conventional method. You must try something that has not yet been tried.

"You shall not succeed by throwing him into a burning

furnace, for this is what was done to Chananyah, Mishael and Azaryah, and they were saved.

"Nor can you throw him into a lion's den. That was done to Daniel and he, too, escaped his fate.

"Imprisonment won't be effective for their ancestor, Yosef, won his freedom from jail.

"Putting him into a copper drum and lighting a fire under him will not work. That is what happened to King Menashe, but, when he prayed to *Hashem*, he was rescued.

"Are you thinking of abandoning him in the desert? Mordechai's forefathers lived in the desert for forty years without mishap. They overcame all the natural hardships and even multiplied!

"Would you blind him? Don't forget Samson, who succeeded in killing more Philistines when he was blinded than when he had his sight.

"The only thing left for you to try is the gallows. No one has yet escaped the fate of hanging." (*Esther Rabbah 9*)

Ready and Waiting

Haman prepared the gallows. He chopped down a cedar from the king's garden and brought it home amidst dancing and singing. He then erected it and said, "Tomorrow at dawn I will hang Mordechai upon this tree."

When Haman set up the gallows, he measured himself against it to see if it was high enough. A Heavenly echo then declared, "It suits you perfectly. It has been ready and waiting since the beginning of Creation!" (*Esther Rabbah 9*)

Shushan Purim. On this day in 5613 (1853), R' Chaim Soloveitchik was born. He served as the rabbi of Brisk and the *rosh yeshivah* of Volozhin. R' Chaim, who died on the 21st of *Av*, 5678 (1918), was one of the most famous figures in the Jewish world.

The Victors

*I*t was *Purim* in Volozhin. A group of secular Jews had gathered to make a mock *Purim* play based upon the weekly portion of *Shoftim* which enumerated all the exemptions from the (Jewish) army allowed a Jew. In their heart of hearts, they longed for the good days when they had been part of the Jewish scene . . .

The scene depicted a large army, supposedly of one hundred thousand soldiers, prepared to go to war. Along came the commander and announced: "Whoever built a house and did not yet dedicate it is exempt from serving in the army."

Ten thousand soldiers stepped out of line and left the camp to return to their homes.

The commander announced: "Whoever planted a vineyard and did not yet redeem its first fruits is exempt from serving."

Another ten thousand soldiers broke rank and left for their homes.

The commander made a third announcement, "Whoever

R' Chaim Soloveitchik

betrothed a woman and did not yet marry her may return home."

Another ten thousand left the rows of soldiers.

While they were still visible in the distance, the commander announced: "Whoever is fearful and meek of heart may return home."

Bedlam reigned. All of the remaining soldiers began running as fast as they could. All except four louts dressed up as great Jewish leaders. One of them in the guise of the *Shaagas Aryeh*, another as the *Noda BeYehudah*, a third as the *Pnei Yehoshua* and a fourth as the *Gaon* of Vilna.

The play was over.

When R' Chaim Soloveitchik was told about this *shpiel* (play), he said, "The fools did not realize that they had not yet finished the play. They forgot the ending. When everything was said and done, these four men alone won the war!"

16 Adar

The day after *Shushan Purim*. The following is told about R' Moshe Isserlis, the Rama, who wrote a commentary on R' Yosef Karo's *Shulchan Aruch*. The Rama was born in 5280 (1520) and died on the eighteenth of *Iyar*, 5332 (1572).

The Thirty-Third Praise

*T*he Rama wrote thirty-three works and served as rabbi of Cracow for thirty-three years. He died on *Lag B'Omer* — the thirty-third day of the Counting of the *Omer*.

At his funeral, one of his most outstanding disciples began enumerating his master's praises: He was brilliant in depth and scope, master of many disciples, generous in charity, hospitable, etc. He reached a count of thirty-two praises and was looking for a thirty-third, but was unsuccessful. This distressed him deeply.

The Rama's *shammash* approached him and said, "I know of yet another tribute to our master. You all know that it is customary to begin the *Purim* feast late in the afternoon and continue on into the night. Each year when it turned dark, the Rama would stop in the middle of his feast to go from house to house reminding people, "Don't forget *Maariv!*" He feared that people might drink themselves into a stupor and the evening prayer would slip their mind. We see that even during the joyous occasion of the *Purim* feast, our master did not cease to worry about his flock." Thus did the *shammash* supply the thirty-third praise of a rabbi who served his people for thirty-three years.

A Special Child

R' Menachem Mendel of Kotzk was the father-in-law of R' Avraham of Sochachov who was born in 5599 (1839) and died on the tenth of *Adar* of 5670 (1910).

He often praised his son-in-law saying, "Do you know why the Bialer *Rebbe* had so fine a son as R' Avraham? One *Purim*, all of the upright and pious men were preoccupied with the festive meal, which is a commandment of the day. The only person in the entire world who was studying Torah was the Bialer *Rebbe*." The Kotzker *Rebbe* would become excited when he reached this part of the tale. "Just imagine that! Had it not been for that one *tzaddik*, the entire world would have been bereft of the study of Torah! Heaven rewarded him with a son who would illuminate the entire world with his Torah and holiness!"

On this day in 5677 (1917), R' Yitzchak of Boyan passed away. The *Rebbe* of the thousands of Boyaner *chasidim* was born on the second day of *Rosh Hashanah* in 5610 (1849). He was a paragon of the finest of virtues and his sanctity was hailed when he was a mere youngster. People would refer to him as *Pachad Yitzchak*.

Thought is Equal to Deed

T he *chasid's* excitement knew no bounds. He was about to meet his saintly *Rebbe*, R' Yitzchak of Boyan, and gaze upon his holy face. Seven years had passed since he had last seen him. Was this not an occasion for eager anticipation and joy?

But his joy was mingled with sadness. For all those long years he had not had the privilege of being elevated by the *Rebbe's* presence.

These emotions filled his heart when he stood before the door of the *Rebbe's* room, waiting to enter.

The creaking of the hinge broke his train of thought. Trembling with awe, he entered the room. His eyes were immediately drawn to the *Rebbe's* glowing countenance which bathed his entire being with waves of radiance and holiness. Then he heard the *Rebbe* speak to him:

"You have not been here for three years!"

The *chasid* was puzzled. What did the *Rebbe* mean? It was seven years since his foot had last stepped over the threshold.

When the *chasid* left the room, he made way to the study of the *Rebbe's* oldest son, R' Menachem Nachum.

The *chasid* extended his hand in greeting and was shocked to hear the same thing. R' Menachem Nachum said, "It's been three years since we saw you last."

The *chasid* was unable to contain his bewilderment and burst out, "I don't understand. It has been seven years since I was last here, not three. How did you make such a mistake?"

R' Menachem Nachum looked straight at the chasid and seemed to ponder the matter. Then he said, "Tell me, did you not plan a trip here three years ago?"

The *chasid* thought back and tried to remember. Slowly, the fog of forgetfulness was somewhat dispelled and a picture emerged.

"Yes, yes!" he said with great excitement. "I had intended to visit the *Rebbe*. I even bought a train ticket, but, for some reason, I had to cancel my plans. I remember how deeply disappointed I was then."

"Let me tell you, then, that when a Jew decides to visit the *Rebbe*, the *Rebbe* already makes contact with him and begins carrying him on his shoulders, so to speak."

Rescue Him from Perdition

The family was seated around the table for supper. "Where is Shmuel?" the master of the house asked his wife, who was busy serving the food.

"I don't know," she replied with a sigh. "Lately, he has been spending a lot of time outside. Something tells my mother's heart that his goings are not for the best purpose."

"What makes you say that?" the father asked, "Why should you suspect him of anything wrong?"

The mother sighed deeply and said, "When he returns home at night, he refuses to tell me where he spent so many hours. I am really very worried about his strange behavior. Yesterday he got up late and I don't know where he could have found a *minyan* at such a late hour. Nor did the fact of not praying with a congregation disturb him in the least!"

Her voice dropped to a whisper so that the other children would not hear, "My heart tells me that he has strayed from the right path. Some terrible turmoil is taking place in his soul. Oh, I wish I were mistaken!"

"What are you saying?" the father said in alarm. "I had no inkling."

Shmuel had been standing behind the door, eavesdropping. He had heard all that his parents had said about him.

"This is the time for me to enter and remove the mask," he said to himself. "I will be frank and honest with my parents and tell them exactly how things stand with me. The groundwork has already been laid. They already sense that I have changed." Shmuel opened the door and stood facing his anxious parents. The mother looked at him with damp eyes.

"Shmuel, where are you coming from at this late hour?" the father asked his son pointedly.

Instead of a reply, Shmuel turned to his mother and said, "Mother, I am hungry."

"Then 'wash' and come to the table," she said, without even turning to look at him.

"I will sit down to eat but I refuse to wash my hands," he said brazenly. "Why should I? My hands are clean."

Without even waiting for the family's reaction of horror and anger, a response which was inevitable, he took a seat and began gulping down his food ravenously.

"Leave the table at once!" the father shouted. "I will not let you eat at my table without first washing and saying the blessing!

"Are you a *goy*, unused to observing our commandments? You should be ashamed of yourself, a boy of fifteen!"

"Don't get so excited! Don't be overly dramatic!" Shmuel said, trying to appease his father. He realized that he had gone too far.

"If you insist, I'll go and wash. I only wanted to say how I felt about things." He got up, went over to the sink and washed his hands as he always had.

He quickly finished his meal, then rose from the table and went to bed, leaving the rest of the family in a state of shock.

The parents were aghast by the events of the evening and could not sleep a wink all that night.

"Our son is lost! He has left us forever," the father wept. "We no longer have any control over him. He is not afraid of us. A boy of his age does not really need his parents any more. He is on his own, free to do as he likes. We had a fine son. Now we have lost him!"

"Don't talk like that, my dear husband! One should never give up hope. We must pray to *Hashem* to make our son come to his senses."

The next morning the family saw that Shmuel's bed was empty. He was gone.

His little sister was the only one who knew anything about his sudden flight. But it was difficult extracting any information from her.

Finally, she said between sobs, "Shmulik is a bad boy, isn't he? He said he would beat me if I cried and all I wanted to do was to tell you that he was taking the two large suitcases with many, many things in it. He took the new briefcase that father bought me." She now burst into heavy weeping. "But it's mine, all mine! Why did he take it?"

The family was shocked to hear the little girl's story. There was no doubt that he had left them for good.

The parents wandered around the house in a daze, not knowing what to do. They could only weep over their tragedy.

The long, troubled day finally came to an end. Night drew its curtain over the world, bringing blackness and gloom.

That evening brought tidings of Job, a tale of misery.

When the children went to bed they found a letter near Shmulik's bed. It told them what they could not have imagined . . .

The mother did not even have the strength to read it to the end. When she came to the lines that said, "And now, I am on my way to the monastery where I will be converted," she suddenly felt her head swim and her knees buckle under her. She fell to the ground in a faint.

She awoke, clutching the letter in her hand. She tore it, again and again, then burst into hysterical tears, expressing the pain of a parent who has lost her son in tragic circumstances.

The father returned home and found his wife sobbing bitterly. When he heard the details of their misfortune, he stood petrified; two tears rolled down his cheeks.

With a quavering hand, he ripped his clothing in mourning.

"My son, my son!" he wept from the depths of his heart. "No! You are my son no longer. And I am not your father. You are dead to me. I must sit in mourning over you and forget you forever!"

"Don't . . . don't," cried the shaken mother. "Don't say such things. One must never lose hope. Even if the point of a sword is thrust at a person's throat, he must never despair of Heavenly mercy. Tomorrow, with the help of *Hashem*, I will visit the Boyaner *Rebbe*, R' Yitzchak. He will help us and in his merit we will be saved."

The next morning she set out on her way to the *tzaddik*. Throughout the journey she prayed with all her heart.

When she entered the *Rebbe's* room, all of her despair seemed to clear away like a departing cloud of smoke. Hope took its place in her heart.

The *tzaddik's* face was suffused with grief when he heard the tragedy of the woman standing before him. He was thoughtful for a few moments and then spoke: "Do you know exactly where your son is at the moment?" he asked.

"Yes, he is in the monastery."

"Then do not tarry. Go there as quickly as you can. Stand by the entrance and shout out my name and my mother's name."

The woman's eyes lit up. With new hope in her heart, she hurried home to tell her husband what the *Rebbe* had said and then rushed off to the monastery.

It was a towering, forbidding structure. Black-shrouded figures flitted somberly past her and were swallowed up through the massive portal of the church. Some stopped to look at the Jewish woman, but then continued on their way. The atmosphere sent chills up and down her back. She thought of returning, but she remembered the *Rebbe's* words and stood like a soldier at her post.

Then, for a moment the courtyard became empty. The woman summoned up her courage and shouted the *Rebbe's* name and his mother's name with all her might. Once, twice, her voice echoed from the huge, ominous walls.

All was still. The woman remained standing there, shivering in the evening cold. Her mother's heart would not let her leave the place, until she saw some favorable omen, although she had accomplished her mission.

An hour passed and then another. She stood there, still nailed to the spot, unable to tear her gaze away from the forbidding building — towering haughty and arrogant — the

building which had swallowed up her oldest son.

Evening turned into night. The world was wrapped in a cloak of ebony. The night and cold drove the last of the pedestrians off the streets, leaving her there alone, waiting, waiting, not knowing exactly what to expect.

The clock struck ten, when surrendering to the night, she, finally, decided to return home, for it was dangerous to be out so late. Those living inside the monastery might become suspicious and do her harm.

With one lingering, longing look, she turned to go, disappointed that she had, as yet, not accomplished anything.

But even during these difficult moments, she did not lose her faith. She was certain that the *Rebbe's* name would have had an effect, if not an immediate one. She would wait patiently.

It was now the father's turn to stand at the entrance to the monastery to wait and watch. He took along several friends and made his way to the spot.

Hours of suspense and expectation passed. The men waited at their post, not knowing exactly what they were waiting for.

They had already decided that there was no sense in standing idly by, indefinitely. They would return home and *Hashem* would effect the miracle in whichever way He desired.

The father, however, decided to remain on guard throughout that night.

As soon as the group of men were somewhat distant, they heard a thud. They turned around and saw a frightening-looking object had fallen from a window onto the ground.

It was a bundle, the size of a large suitcase; it had fallen without shattering. They heaved a sigh of relief. But, then, the bundle began writhing and squirming, like a lumbering bear.

Off came the white outer covering and then successive layers. Finally, something stood up on two feet; it was a young boy. He looked at the men, tears glistening in his eyes.

"Let's get out of here, quickly!" the boy said urgently.

"I want to go home before it is too late and they come after us!"

They no longer harbored any doubts. The figure dressed in black was the lost apostate-to-be son. And he wanted to return home!

They were bewildered, but they supported him and helped him. He was bruised and ached from the fall. They fled as quickly as they could.

When they felt they were safe, they slowed down their pace and relaxed. Shmuel was still overwrought and unable to open his mouth. Later, when they reached home, he recovered enough from the shock to relate all that had happened.

"They showered me with honor and promises without end. They praised me for having freely chosen to convert to Christianity. I already imagined a rosy future in which I figured as a prominent and wealthy person. Then, suddenly, for no reason that I can explain, strange feelings stirred within me. I felt melancholy; remorse gnawed at me, ruining my joy. I became so restless that I did not know what to do with myself. I never had such strong emotions before. My conscience weighed heavily upon me, like a mountain, but there was no place to which I could escape. I wanted to flee, to run away from my own thoughts. My anguish grew from moment to moment, piercing my heart like a sharp dagger. I saw your dear figures, father and mother; your faces would not leave me. How could I be so cruel to you, who loved me so dearly!

"Worst of all was the remorse I felt for having ever thought of leaving my faith and heritage, the source of eternal life. I was forfeiting both worlds in one stroke! Riches were nothing, I realized, in the face of the true satisfaction gained from doing just one *mitzvah*.

"During these moments of truth I felt myself to be the most miserable creature on earth. I wanted to retract everything, but the gates of the monastery were locked and bolted. I could never escape. I could never return to my home, to my people.

"I was lost.

"Suddenly, I thought to myself that death was better than a life like this! And I made a daring decision. I would jump from the window. If G-d willed, I would remain alive. If not, at least I would die as a Jew and thus atone for my sin.

"I bolted the door of the room from the inside, put on priests' clothing as a disguise and covered my face with a stocking. As an extra precaution, I wrapped a white sheet around myself to scare people into thinking that I was a ghost.

"Then I cast my lot with *Hashem* and, as you see, was saved by a miracle.

"For it was a miracle that my body was not shattered by the fall. The sudden return to my senses was a second miracle."

The son finished his tale. His eyes met those of his mother. Both of them thanked *Hashem* for the double miracle. But although the boy did not, the mother did, indeed, know what lay behind the miracles. She knew in whose merit he had found his way back — through that of the *Rebbe* of Boyan.

On this day in 5554 (1794), R' Alexander Ziskind passed away in Horodna, Lithuania. He was the author of *Yesod Veshoresh Ha'avodah* and a unique man of great renown.

If R' Alexander Lived in Our Generation

R' Alexander Ziskind once came to visit R' Dov Ber, the *Maggid* of Mezeritch, the direct successor of the Baal Shem Tov. He wanted to learn his ways and become one of his avowed followers.

But the *Maggid* of Mezeritch refused to accept him as a student. "You don't need me," he said. "You have attained all that *Chasidus* has to offer on your own!"

Indeed, many stories are told of R' Alexander's fervor in prayer. R' Nachum of Horodna, one of his outstanding disciples, was fond of telling one in particular:

A distinguished guest once spent a *Shabbos* with R' Nachum.

Friday night. The prayers were already long over, but R' Nachum had not yet come home.

Many hours passed before they finally heard his steps approaching. He had been busy finding families willing to take in Jewish soldiers serving in the Czar's army who had arrived in Horodna for *Shabbos*. Only after all of them had been placed did R' Nachum return home to make *kiddush* and eat the *Shabbos* meal.

R' Nachum was deeply distressed that his esteemed guest had waited so long without eating.

In order to appease him, lest he be angry, R' Nachum said, "Listen to me, my dear guest, while I tell you what R' Alexander used to do. Each Friday, he would wash hands, face and feet and immerse himself in a *mikveh*. Then he would put on his *Shabbos* clothing and turn to the *beis knesses*. He carried a parchment scroll of *Shir HaShirim* which he had written himself. He would read it in the synagogue with fervor and ardor. It was said that the angels themselves would stand by to listen to his *Shir HaShirim* which went straight to Heaven.

" 'In previous generations, rabbis were able to do this. But they did not have the responsibility of seeing to the welfare of Jewish soldiers. I am certain that if R' Alexander were alive in this generation, he would not hesitate for a moment, but would forego saying the *Shir HaShirim* and rush out to help a Jewish soldier who was looking for a place for *Shabbos*!' "

The Power of Prayer

A wandering beggar was once found on the crossroads leading to Horodna, suffering from the bitter cold. Kind people brought him to the *beis medrash* and tried to warm him.

R' Alexander Ziskind turned to the people caring for him and said, "Why do you labor so hard? Just recite the prayer of

Nishmas kol chai of the *Shabbos* morning service. I have no doubt that the very fervor with which you say that prayer will bring him to himself!"

On this day in 5569 (1809), R' Meir Leibush ben Yechiel Michel, the Malbim, was born. The Malbim was famed as a great sage and leader. He died on the first of *Tishrei* in 5640 (1879).

No Need for Experts

The Reform movement convened in Brunsweig to discuss changes in Jewish law and practice; they invited the Malbim to attend.

He came and, in his turn, addressed the audience: "When a king wishes to build a magnificent palace, he hires the best engineers, architects and laborers. However, when he needs to demolish a palace, he only requires rough, brawny men, for their brute force.

"The King of kings built a splendid palace, the Torah. He engaged the best minds to construct it, beginning with Moshe and continuing on with the *tannaim* and *amoraim*, up to the sages of our present day. You now propose to demolish this structure. I ask you: why do you need 'rabbis' for that task? That is completely unnecessary. All you need do is call in some ignoramuses and louts from the marketplace and they will do the job far more efficiently."

With these words, he rose and left the hall.

Identical Question — With a Great Difference

In a speech, the Malbim quoted verses from *Daniel* to prove that the time of the Redemption was near.

A man from the audience arose and said, "But our Sages warned us against reckoning the time of the Redemption!"

The Malbim replied with a story:

Two villagers — a father and son — once traveled to a fair in a big city. When they had left their small village, the son asked his father, "When will we arrive?" "Fool! We just left our house," the father said angrily, "and already you are pestering me with your questions of when we will arrive?"

Many days passed and they still had not reached their destination. The son heard his father turn to the wagoner and ask, "When will we reach the big city?" The son was surprised and said, "When I asked that question you scolded me. Why do you now ask it, yourself?"

"You asked the question at the very beginning of our journey," said the father, "when it was meaningless. But now that we have been traveling for a long while, it is not a foolish question at all!"

"So, too," the Malbim explained, "when we first went into exile, we were forbidden to calculate the date of the Redemption, lest we fall into despair. But much time has

ר׳ מֵאִיר לֵיבּוּשׁ מַלְבִּים ·
קעניגסבערגער רב

elapsed since then and there is no doubt that our Deliverance
is at hand. Now it is permissible to reckon the time left until
the Redeemer comes."

On this day in 5400 (1640), R' Yoel Sirkis passed away. R' Yoel was one of the great leaders of our people. His works *(Bayis Chadash)* served as basic halachic texts for his and future generations.

Child Prodigy

E ven as a child of tender years, R' Yoel Sirkis had already gained a reputation as a genius, a child blessed with many talents. He dazzled his teachers, the great scholars of Lublin, with his brilliance.

The Maharshal, R' Shlomo Luria, heard of the prodigy, and invited him to 'speak in learning'. The two enjoyed a lively dialogue. The Maharshal was so taken by the child that he allowed Yoel to be called up in his *beis medrash* for the *haftorah* portion of the festival, even though the boy was very young — many years before his thirteenth birthday.

One day the boy's teacher taught him the verse in *parashas Va'era* which reads, "This time I am sending all of my plagues . . ." Rashi comments: "This teaches us that the plague of the firstborn was as harsh as all the others combined." The teacher presented the question which bothered the commentators. The plague referred to here was that of hail and not of the firstborn. Why, then, did Rashi mention the last plague which was not yet due?

The teacher gave a contrived explanation, but little Yoel

had a better answer. His eyes sparkling, he said, "Perhaps Rashi originally wrote the *rashei tevos*, an abbreviation, *mem-beis*, referring to *makas barad*, the hail. A copyist, then, mistakenly expanded the abbreviation to read *makas bechoros*."

His Greatness and His Humility

The boy matured early in both Torah knowledge and good deeds. He was acknowledged as a leader of the generation while yet a young man.

His fame spread throughout the land and offers for the post of rabbi reached him from illustrious and distant cities. He chose to make his home in Lubomel, Poland. But to the dismay of the communal leaders of that city and of all its residents, he did not remain there long.

Lubomel possessed a worthy Torah scholar who studied day and night, but shied away from recognition. He lived in dire poverty, and no one was aware of his desperate plight.

The new rabbi, however, took note of this modest scholar and befriended him. He even helped him occasionally with money. This man once gave the rabbi some of his writings to study and to comment upon. The rabbi took them home with him, promising him to look at them that evening. Later, when he sat down to devote his attention to the writings, R' Yoel was overwhelmed by the vast scholarship of this unassuming scholar. He pored over the writings all that night, wondering how this man had remained so obscure and unknown when he was so brilliant. On the morrow, he summoned all of the leaders of the community and told them of his discovery. He then said, "You deserve strong rebuke for letting such a situation arise. This great man has been living in your midst for many years. He is a *tzaddik* and a *gaon*, worthy of serving in the most prestigious of Jewish communities, but you have ignored him all these years. He is truly fitting to serve as the *av beis din* here and any other rabbi whom you invite can be considered guilty of usurping his right."

Having had his say, R' Yoel tendered his resignation and demanded that the trustees appoint the obscure scholar, their fellow townsman, in his stead.

His Mother's Son

R' Shmuel Yaffe, father of the noted R' Yoel Sirkis, was numbered among the most prominent men of Lublin. But the wheel of fortune turned for him and he lost his immense wealth. He became so poor that the family was on the verge of starvation.

R' Shmuel's worthy wife, Sor'ke, could not bear to see her family suffering. It pained her heart to send little Yoel off to *cheder* each day without as much as a crust of bread. And so, she decided to take matters into hand and engage in business. She opened up a fabric store to support her learned husband and brilliant son.

Heaven rewarded her for her sacrifice. When Yoel grew up to become a great man, people appended his mother's name to his. Thus, instead of referring to him as R' Yoel Yaffe, they called him R' Yoel Sirkis, that is 'Sor'ke's', to commemorate his valorous mother.

R' Elimelech of Lizensk passed away on this day in 5546 (1786). A man of G-d and a great leader. His work, *Noam Elimelech*, is one of the basic texts on *Chasidus* and mystic wisdom.

I Am to Blame

The home of R' Elimelech of Lizensk was always bustling with activity. Hundreds of people passed through it at all times, be it to study Torah under him, to receive a blessing for health, *parnasah*, children, or to ask the *Rebbe* to pray and save them from whatever danger faced them.

R' Elimelech would look at the throngs that filled his house and say, "They are justified in coming here and making many demands on me, for health, livelihood and so on. For I am the one to blame for their hardship!"

"The *Rebbe* is to blame?" his listeners would wonder. "How is that possible?"

"Yes, indeed," he would explain. "The world is evenly balanced; half is righteous and half is sinful. I, with my many sins, tip the scale down on the debit side and thus cause good people to suffer. Therefore, they are right to demand that I give them children, grant them health or provide them with means of livelihood. 'You are to blame' they say, in so many words. 'Therefore, at least pray for us!' "

R' Elimelech is Surprised

R' Elimelech of Lizensk was once walking along a road when he met a young man carrying a bundle.

"Where are you going?" he asked.

"I am going to visit R' Michele of Zolochov," he replied.

"That surprises me, young man," he said.

"Indeed? Why?" the young man asked in wonder.

R' Elimelech explained: "When I was younger, I also wanted to visit R' Michele, the *Maggid* of Zolochov, and when I heard that he was to pass through a city near Lizensk, I seized the opportunity to see him.

"I went to that city and approached one of the houses in the Jewish neighborhood. All the houses were empty. I went from one to another until I found an old woman busy cooking. "Where has everyone gone?' I asked in surprise.

"She replied, 'R' Michele of Zolochov is in town and has announced a 'Yom Kippur' today. He is revealing everyone's sins from the day he was born up to the present. If you want to know where everyone is, go to the *beis knesses* where they are all gathered in prayer.'

"When I heard her words, I began trembling all over. My teeth chattered and my hair stood on end. I was afraid that R' Michele would tell me all the sins I had committed during my lifetime. I left the old woman's house and ran back home to Lizensk.

"And now," concluded R' Elimelech, "I can't help wondering how you, young man, are not afraid to approach a man as holy and far seeing as R' Michele!"

During these days, Jews all over the world are approached for *kimcha d'Pischa*, charity for Passover, to help the poor buy provisions for *Pesach*.

One Favor at a Time

R' Yosef Dov Soloveitchik of Brisk, besides being an outstanding scholar devoted to the study of the Torah, was also deeply involved in public matters. He would walk great distances to raise money for institutions of Torah and charity and labor for them with a holy zeal and enthusiasm.

Once he arrived at the home of a wealthy resident of Brisk to collect charity.

The master of the house greeted him warmly, as befitted the rabbi's station. When he was told the purpose of the visit, he said respectfully, "But the rabbi knows that for many years I have been actively involved in communal matters. Whenever I am asked to come or help, I do so without hesitation. Why, then, did you have to come in person, this time?"

The host was moved as he said those words, but even more so was R' Yosef Dov in hearing them. He was silent for a moment, then said, "It is true that the rabbi's dignity should require people to come to him whenever something important arises. But the Sages of ancient times ruled that in time of need,

R' Yosef Dov Soloveitchik

one must set aside the honor due him. In this, they relied upon
the verse, 'When it is necessary to act for *Hashem*, they set
aside Your Torah' *(Tehillim 119:126)*.

"I thought that if I asked you to come to me, that would be
asking a favor of you. This would have undoubtedly harmed
the worthy cause for which I am now collecting. For it would
have been difficult to ask for a contribution. It is not fair to ask
one favor after another.

"I, therefore, troubled myself to come to you. This way, I
am only asking one favor — to give generously for the
important communal institution in our city."

The rabbi's reply deeply affected the host, who was already
moved. He gave more than he had ever given before.

On this day in 5626 (1866), R' Yitzchak Meir of Ger passed away. The Chidushei HaRim was born in 5559 (1799) and was the first of the illustrious Gerrer dynasty.

A Tzaddik in Prison

Throughout the years that Jews lived in Poland, they were recognizably different from their gentile neighbors. They wore different clothing and let their beards and *peyos* grow long.

In 5611 (1851) the government passed a law forbidding Jews to wear their distinguishing clothing and required them to shave off their beards and sidelocks, so that they would look like all other Poles.

The government had publicized the new regulations previously, but they were only to go into effect as law in that year.

In its first stage, it was to apply only to the Jews of Warsaw; later it would include those of other cities and towns throughout Poland.

When the designated day arrived, most Jews simply ignored the law and did nothing about changing their appearance. "Our clothing, beard and *peyos* distinguish us from the gentiles. We will not let the government touch them!" they vowed.

The Warsaw police were issued orders to arrest anyone in Jewish dress or with beard or *peyos* — and to forcibly shave them.

The police went out to the streets to see if they could 'catch' any traditional-looking Jews. Many Jews protested violently when the police sought to shave off their beards. There were fights which ended with Jews being thrown into jail.

Warsaw seethed. Its Jewish neighborhood were filled with the cries of Jews struggling against arrest and the weeping of families whose menfolk had already been imprisoned.

The word spread that the police were laying an ambush for the *Rebbe*, R' Yitzchak Meir of Ger, himself! At that time, he was living in Warsaw. Rumor had it that the police aimed to catch the *Rebbe* and shave off his beard! People whispered that the *maskilim*, those who had thrown off the yoke of Torah, were behind the idea. They had suggested to the authorities that once the *Rebbe's* beard was forcibly shorn off, Jews would no longer protest against the decree.

The *Rebbe* heard the talk and left his home secretly. He went to live elsewhere until the danger passed.

The prominent members of the chasidic community decided to visit the chief of police. They begged him not to touch the *Rebbe*. Upon his guarantee that nothing would happen, the *Rebbe* returned to his home.

But he was still uneasy. His fears caused the *Rebbe* to change his name from Rotenberg to Alter, the surname which the Gerrer dynasty bears to this very day.

When a few months passed and the Warsaw police saw that they were fighting a losing battle, that the Jews would fight tooth and nail for their right to dress as tradition demanded, their zeal faded. In truth, they had not expected such resistance and it had worn them down. They became very lax in enforcing the law.

The *maskilim* noticed this and were irked. They went to the minister of police and pointed out to him that the police of Warsaw were not enforcing the new law and were looking the other way. "The rich *chasidim* must have bribed the police," they claimed. "This is making a mockery of the Polish government!"

"And what do you suggest that we do about it?" the minister asked. He assumed that they had a plan up their sleeves, and he was right. "You must force the Gerrer *Rebbe* to issue a proclamation to his flock that Jews must keep the law since their Torah obligates a Jew to accept the authority of his country of residence."

One of them added, "The *Rebbe's* word is law to all of his chasidim. They will obey him to the letter, old and young. All other rabbis have already submitted to this law, all except for the Gerrer *Rebbe*, who refused to bend!"

"And if he continues to object," another suggested, "he should be thrown into jail until he changes his mind and becomes tractable."

This idea pleased the minister who was no friend of the Jews. He issued an immediate order for the imprisonment of the *Rebbe*. He knew that if the police came to take their leader away, the community would protest violently and might even riot. He therefore decided to pay him a midnight visit. He came with a warrant of arrest and led the *Rebbe* to a waiting carriage which drove him to the prison.

A group of ministers and officials awaited his arrival. They surrounded him and demanded that he issue a call for all Jews to obey the new law — to adopt modern dress and shave off their beards.

"I refuse," said the *Rebbe*.

"We will give you two days time. If you do not issue such a letter by then, we will forcibly shave off your beard," they warned him.

"You will be waiting in vain," said R' Yitzchak Meir. "I will never give in, not even on one hair. I maintain that it is forbidden for a Jew to obey these laws; whatever your schemes they will come to naught. I will not budge."

The men gathered there realized that the *Rebbe* meant what he said and that nothing they did to him would make him change his mind. He was firm as a rock. They put him in a cell together with hardened criminals and locked the door behind them.

As soon as the *Rebbe* entered, he became the focus of a dozen stares. These prisoners were not accustomed to such a cell-mate. After they recovered from the initial shock, their leader approached the *Rebbe* and said, "There is an unwritten law here that when a new prisoner enters the cell, he must obey whatever the veterans tell him to do. If he refuses, he must serve all of the prisoners until the next newcomer arrives. You are not exempt from this custom."

"What must I do?" the *Rebbe* asked.

One of the prisoners left the group and lay down on the floor. The others explained that he must sit on him.

"I refuse to do that," the *Rebbe* said. "I refuse to sit on the body of another Jew, no matter who."

"But those are your orders!" everyone clamored.

"And if you refuse to obey," the leader added, "you will be persecuted. We will not give you a moment's rest."

The *Rebbe* was not alarmed by these threats. "I refuse to sit upon another Jew!" he said emphatically.

A voice arose from the ground. It was the prisoner stretched out on the floor. He begged the *Rebbe* to fulfill the orders. "If you refuse, I will suffer along with you. You cannot imagine how they torture you, here," he added.

Only then, when helping a fellow Jew was involved, did the *Rebbe* agree to sit upon the prisoner for a few moments. And they, then, left him alone.

If the Polish ministers thought that imprisoning the *Rebbe* at night would prevent an uproar among the Jews, they were sorely mistaken. The news spread throughout the city. Thousands of Warsaw Jews did not sleep that night. The city simmered and boiled. The prominent Jews labored incessantly to try to have the Rebbe released from jail.

The Kotzker *chasidim* in Warsaw sent a special delegation to their *Rebbe*. To their surprise, when they arrived in Kotzk and told the *Rebbe* of R' Yitzchak Meir's imprisonment, he was not at all alarmed or surprised. Serenely and calmly, he sat down to write a letter to the *chasidim* in Warsaw reassuring them that they need not worry for the *Rebbe's* welfare. The government officials would never be able to touch his beard. On the contrary, his imprisonment would bring great benefit to all of Jewry, for the law would be revoked.

Meanwhile, the Jews of Warsaw were anxious and overwrought. The turmoil in the city grew from hour to hour. By morning, the streets were filled with throngs of people, numbering in the thousands, who could only talk about the shocking event. It was interesting to note that even Jews who had abandoned Jewish practice were also shaken by the event and went to protest it.

A large group formed near the prison. The sound of their weeping and praying filled the air. The size of the tremendous crowd did not escape the notice of the ministers. When the minister of police who had arrested the *Rebbe* saw what a protest he had aroused, he became alarmed. He had never dreamed that the arrest would cause a riot. That morning he was visited by a delegation of Jewish dignitaries who were joined by some Polish noblemen. They all expressed their shock that such a personage as the holy *Rebbe* of Ger, leader of thousands, should be imprisoned in such an enlightened city as Warsaw.

The minister was taken aback by the extreme reaction

which his act had evoked and was forced to promise to free the *Rebbe* at once.

Before noon that day, the Chidushei HaRim was released and sent home.

R' Yitzchak Meir of Ger was freed, but the shocking event left a mark upon Warsaw Jewry. What especially rankled them was the fact that several of their own, 'enlightened' Jews, had had a significant role in that chapter. Some people were even able to point a finger at the guilty ones who were directly responsible for the *Rebbe's* imprisonment.

Small wonder, then, that a virulent controversy broke out in Warsaw between the orthodox circles and the freethinking *maskilim*. Many Jews vowed to avenge the Rebbe's honor upon the guilty ones and they began persecuting them mercilessly.

When the *maskilim* saw this difficult state they began to spread new slander day after day against the observant Jews, hoping thereby to gain the protection of the government.

The controversy continued to rage. R' Yitzchak Meir was fully aware of it. He decided that it would not die down until he left the city.

When the prominent men of the community learned of his decision, they begged the *Rebbe* to reconsider. It was shortly before *Pesach*, they reminded him, and the Festival without the *Rebbe* would be unbearable.

But the *Rebbe* was determined. He left Warsaw at the end of *Adar* and moved to Novidbur. The Jews of Warsaw were heartbroken. Instead of feeling like a prince on the Festival of Liberation, the *Rebbe* would be in exile, far from his city and his home. Before leaving Warsaw, the *Rebbe* declared that he would not return until the government repealed the discriminatory law.

The Jews of Novidbur, however, were overjoyed to have a *tzaddik* in their midst. The entire city turned out to welcome him and escort him to the luxurious apartment which they had prepared in his honor.

When he reached his lodgings, he seemed very pleased with what he saw. He turned to the throngs which encircled him from all sides and said, "The name of your city, Novidbur, means 'a new courtyard'. It will be good to think new Torah thoughts in this city! This is what R' Yehudah Hanassi referred to when he asked, 'What is a new court?' and R' Yochanan replied, 'A place where new concepts were formed' (*Yevamos 7b*)."

R' Yitzchak Meir thought that he would remain in Novidbur over *Pesach* and had already baked *matzos* there. Still, he sensed that his *chasidim* in Warsaw would grieve over his absence, and that would intensify the controversy all the more. He, therefore, sent a letter to his followers in which he begged them not to quarrel or foment ill feelings for his sake. "We are all sons of Avraham, Yitzchak and Yaakov," he wrote to them. "The Torah had no need to remind us to 'love your neighbor' and 'do not hate' since we are all brothers and neighbors."

The *chasidim* read the letter and tried to resign themselves to the fact that their leader would not be with them during the Festival.

Immediately after *Shabbos Hagadol*, the *Shabbos* preceding *Pesach*, the authorities announced that they had repealed the law!

The notables of the Warsaw community hurried to Novidbur to tell the *Rebbe* the good news. When he heard it, R' Yitzchak Meir said, "The time has come to return to Warsaw."

He came back — and the Jews of Warsaw had light and joy!

On this day in 5655 (1895), R' Avraham Yehoshua Heschel Twersky, the *Admor* of Machnovka-Bnei Brak, was born. One of the grandsons of the holy *Maggid* of Chernobyl, he was especially noted for his self-sacrifice for Torah and *mitzvos* in the wastelands of Russia. He was like refreshing dew to the hearts of the depressed. The *Rebbe* died on the eve of *Yom Kippur* 5748 (1987).

A Precious Mitzvah

R' Yehoshua Heschel of Machnovka was the symbol of a Jew who lived a life of self-sacrifice. At a very young age, the halo of holiness and perfection in the observance of *mitzvos* was already apparent.

In 5680 (1920) after the First World War, the Czarist government of Russia was overthrown by the Communists. The new regime suppressed all signs of religion. When the *Rebbe* was caught encouraging the practice of Judaism, he was exiled to Siberia, the land of perpetual ice.

After he was there for a month, on *rosh chodesh Elul* which fell on a *Shabbos*, the commander of the camp where he was interned summoned him, in order to evaluate his work.

The *Rebbe* appeared but when he was asked to sign a declaration, he adamantly refused.

R' Avraham Yehoshua Heschel Twersky, Admor of Machnovka

"Today is *Shabbos!*" he declared. "A Jew is forbidden to write on *Shabbos.*"

The commander was shocked by the audacity of the prisoner.

"Don't you know that you can be shot to death for disobeying such an order?" he fumed.

For some inexplicable reason, he did not shoot him then and there. Instead, he transferred the case of the disobedient prisoner to the district commissioner, General Chenstov himself. Before him, the *Rebbe* refused to sign as well. R' Avraham Yehoshua Heschel was returned to the camp commander. He was to be shot.

The commander gave him another chance and told him to

sign at once. The *Rebbe* unbuttoned his jacket in reply and said, "Shoot! I am ready to sacrifice my life for the sake of the holy Sabbath."

The *Rebbe* of noble countenance was taken to the execution square and led to a wall. At a mere ten meters, the commander took aim and fired.

And then the unexpected happened. The shot backfired. The commander fell to the ground, a bullet in his leg.

The commander understood that the rabbi must be a holy man. He crawled across the frozen ground to the rabbi's feet and confessed that he, too, was a Jew, but an assimilated one. He promised to hide the *Rebbe* and do whatever he asked of him.

"I am not in need of anything," said the *Rebbe*, shrugging off the miracle that had just occurred to him. "But as a Jew, you must surely be aware that the High Holy days are approaching, followed by a Festival which entails many commandments. Do me the kindness of procuring a *shofar* for me for *Rosh Hashanah* and providing a *succah* to sit in during the Festival of *Succos*."

The commander eagerly promised to do this. He had his wound dressed, then returned the *Rebbe* to the camp and provided for all of his strange requests. The *Rebbe* preferred this to having his life made easier at camp by reducing his work load and improving his food rations.

The *Admor* of Machnovka blew the *shofar* on *Rosh Hashanah* and sat in a *succah* on *Succos* even in the frozen hinterland of Siberia.

He remained there for two years and was then released. But this was not to be a final farewell. After a brief sojourn at home he was again sent to the wasteland after the secret police caught him immersing himself in a *mikveh* before *Shabbos*. Thus, he suffered for many years, yet he sacrificed himself for even the small details of a *mitzvah* and did not allow himself any laxness due to his difficult situation. He, finally, was permitted to go up to *Eretz Yisrael* where he settled in Bnei Brak, the city of Torah and *Chasidus*, and reestablished the court of Machnovka.

But throughout his life, even when serenity smiled down upon him in the Holy Land, he did not forget those bitter years during which he had fortified his pure soul. At the end of his days, he once fell ill on *Succos*. His close adherents begged him to forego the requirement of sleeping in the *succah*, since, due to ill health, he was exempt from doing so.

But the *Rebbe* replied indignantly, "When the temperature in Siberia fell to thirty degrees below zero, I slept in the *succah*. Here, where the nights are balmy and pleasant, shall I sleep inside and forego that precious *mitzvah*?"

On this day in 5521 (1761), R' Gershon of Kitov
passed away. A holy and righteous man in his own
right, he was also the brother-in-law of the Baal
Shem Tov. R' Gershon went up to *Eretz Yisrael* in
5506 (1746) upon the request of the Baal Shem Tov.

In and Out of Eretz Yisrael

I t was Friday night in Mezibuz and R' Yisrael was
seated at his table together with his select circle of
chasidim. The atmosphere was sublime and exalted. The
profound thoughts which came forth from his lips
penetrated deeply into the souls of the *chasidim* and drew
them up to Heavenly spheres.

Suddenly, the Baal Shem Tov emitted a deep sigh. "Ah! I
cannot see R' Gershon anywhere in the Holy Land. I have
searched for him, but I cannot find him." He sighed again and
was silent. The rest of the men sighed in sympathy, but did
not ask any questions.

Morning arrived. Again the privileged circle sat around the
Baal Shem Tov's *Shabbos tish*, uplifted and joyous. Delicious
foods were served, enhancing the spiritual and bringing with
them a complete *oneg Shabbos* — joy of the Sabbath.

The group was singing the *Shabbos zemiros* when the voice
of the Baal Shem Tov broke through. "Ah!" he exclaimed
happily. "Now I see R' Gershon in the Holy Land! I was

seeking him, but now I see him!" The *chasidim* shared the *Rebbe's* joy.

That *motzaei Shabbos* the *chasidim* gathered around the *Rebbe* in his private study to ask him what had happened during the day. "How could R' Gershon have disappeared from *Eretz Yisrael* so suddenly?" they asked. "And how could he have returned there so mysteriously in the midst of the holy day?"

The *Rebbe's* face lit up with a knowing smile. But he would not reveal his secret. "Let he himself come and testify to what happened," was all that he said.

The *chasidim* remained puzzled for a long time to come. They could not forget that mysterious scene and discussed it among themselves. Eventually, word of the riddle reached R' Gershon's ears while he was staying in Chevron.

He sent a letter of explanation to his peers in Mezibuz and said, "It is written, 'A light is spread before the *tzaddik'* — nothing is hidden from a *tzaddik*. The truth is that on that *Shabbos* when R' Yisrael mentioned my name in Mezibuz, I was staying in Acco which lies on the northern coast of *Eretz Yisrael*. I reached it after a long, arduous journey, having been invited by one of the prominent men of that community to serve as *sandak* at his infant son's *bris*. There are two synagogues in Acco, one which is within the borders of *Eretz Yisrael* and the other which is technically outside of the area considered holy soil. Since I had no idea of the halachic borderline dividing the holy soil from the unsanctified soil, by error I prayed in the synagogue which was 'outside' of *Eretz Yisrael*. Later, when I found out, I regretted it. On the morrow I prayed in the second synagogue which lay within the designated borders of *Eretz Yisrael*."

Pesach is less than three weeks away.

The Wound and the Matzos

R' Chaim of Brisk told the following story about his father, the famous R' Yosef Dov Soloveitchik, rabbi of Brisk who was born in 5580 (1810) and died on the fourth of *Iyar* of 5562 (1892).

R' Yosef Dov first began serving as rabbi of Brisk shortly before *Pesach*. He had previously lived in Warsaw and wished to bake his *matzos* there. He took his son, R' Chaim, along to Warsaw and they supervised the baking.

When the work was completed, he returned to Brisk while R' Chaim remained behind to transport the *matzos* home and watch over them throughout the journey in accordance with all of the demanding specifications of his scrupulous father.

As soon as he arrived in Brisk, he brought the *matzos* directly to his father and reported on his journey.

"Everything went smoothly, father!" he said. "The *matzos* are perfectly kosher."

His father was uneasy. He felt that something had happened on the trip. He pressed his son, "Tell me, did everything really go smoothly? Nothing happened to the *matzos*?"

"Father, I already told you that everything is *kosher lemehadrin* with regards to the *matzos*."

The Festival passed and R' Yosef Dov again asked his son, "Now you can tell me the truth. What happened to the *matzos*?"

R' Chaim had to confess: "On the way to Brisk, when I was traveling in the train, watching the precious package like the apple of my eye, I kept fearing that I might doze off along the way and leave the *matzos* unguarded.

"In order to prevent this, I wound the end of the string, tied around the box of *matzos*, about my finger as tightly as I could so that the pain would prevent me from falling asleep. But I overdid it and cut my finger. I then poured some salt upon the wound to increase the pain and prevent me from dozing off. This is how I reached Brisk with the package intact," he explained, holding up his finger for his father to see. "The wound has not yet healed!"

In telling this tale, R' Chaim would add, "Had I told my father the story before the Festival, he would not have eaten those *matzos* which had caused a Jew suffering and pain."

To Behold the Holy Labor

R' Yitzchak Zev Soloveitchik, son of R' Chaim of Brisk, was born on *chol hamoed Succos* of 5647 (1887) and died in Jerusalem on *erev Yom Kippur* of 5720 (1959). His *matzah*-baking was a noteworthy event in Jerusalem.

Scholars would discuss every facet of the Brisker *Rav's* baking, deriving many *halachos* from even the slightest of his actions. *Chasidim* and men of note would make every effort to be present when he undertook the holy labor, so as to absorb the atmosphere which surrounded him. Even tender *cheder* children would rush to see the great man baking. The sight of his figure remained etched in their hearts forever more.

Frantic preparations began several weeks before the *yom tov* in R' Yitzchak Zev's home. The first step was procuring *shemurah* flour, but before that, the laws had to be thoroughly clarified. Then the rabbi's representatives went to buy new marble slabs upon which the dough would be rolled. Every other utensil to be used in the baking process was also bought anew each year.

All the equipment was brought to the great man's house and guarded with the utmost heed.

On a Thursday, some of his followers would go out to Motza, a village outside of Jerusalem, to draw the natural water from the clear spring that bubbled forth there.

It was amazing to watch them waiting for the precise moment when, according to the *Rav's* conclusions, they could draw the water. All of the disciples stood poised, their eyes glued to their watches, waiting for the precise moment to start filling the clean vessels used only for this one purpose.

The moment arrived and soon all the utensils were filled. Carefully, they carried them to the bus returning to Jerusalem.

The night before the baking was a night-watch. No one slept. The bakery which was situated in the Beis Yisrael section filled up with Brisker adherents who prepared the place for the baking to take place on the morrow. Everyone worked with amazing dexterity and speed.

The baking began early in the morning. Each person involved had to present himself before the Brisker *Rav* for inspection. He checked their hands and urged them to bake with holy intentions, *leshem matzos mitzvah*.

The air of holiness settled in almost immediately, amidst the feverish activity, long before the tantalizing smell of *matzos* rose up from the oven.

They finally began rolling out the dough. The Brisker *Rav* ran from one room to the next, supervising, examining, keeping an eye on every phase of the work. He was bathed in the fire of holy zeal; his body shook from fear and awe as he kept on repeating, "*Leshem matzos mitzvah* — for the sake of the commanded *matzos*."

The pile of *matzos* rose. Then a recess was called. The dozens of workers halted their labors and stretched their weary limbs; they did not mind this break, knowing that the Brisker *Rav* would pay them for their time regardless.

Meanwhile, the *Rav* went off to say the morning prayers. One hour passed and another. His prayer stretched out. During all this time the bakery was paralyzed for everyone knew that if the Brisker *Rav* was away, the work could not proceed.

A few hours later, when R' Yitzchak Zev finally finished and returned to the bakery, the baking resumed.

This repeated itself, year in and year out. Fortunate are the eyes that witnessed all this!

These are days of preparation for the coming Festival of *Pesach*. Throughout Jewish communities all over the world, synagogue officials collect money for *kimcha d'Pischa*, charity to provide the poor with their holiday needs.

Written in Full

*I*t was a year of severe drought and famine. There was a shortage of wheat, which caused prices to soar.

The communal leaders of Vilna decided that year to reduce the amount allocated to the poor for *kimcha d'Pischa*.

When the Vilna *Gaon* learned of this decision, he called together the wealthy men of the community as well as the charity treasurers who distributed the funds. They all came, not knowing why he had called the meeting.

He began with a Torah thought, then spoke about the approaching Festival. In the course of his address, he took up a volume of *Shemos* and began reading from it, "Seven days shall you eat *matzos* . . . *matzos* shall be eaten for seven days" (13:6,7).

"Do you know," he turned to his audience, "why the word *matzos* appears without the *vav* whereas later it is written fully with the *vav*?"

The men furrowed their brows and sought an answer to the

Gaon's question. He supplied it himself. "The Torah had a special reason for doing so. In the verse, 'You shall eat *matzos*,' '*matzos*' lacks the *vav* to tell you that a person may skimp and save when it comes to what he and his family eats. But with regards to the verse, '*Matzos* shall be eaten,' '*matzos*' is written with the *vav* because you cannot skimp on the food of others, the people who rely on you for help. You must provide the poor with their full measure, just as it is written in full. One must not dream of not giving to the poor what they are accustomed to receive."

During the period of the *tanaim*, this day was considered a *yom tov* because the Jews were then informed that the harsh decrees against them had been revoked. Thanks to the intercession of R' Yehudah ben Shamua and his friends, Jews were once again permitted to study Torah, circumcise their sons and keep the *Shabbos* (*Rosh Hashanah* 19a). As then, Jews throughout the ages have sacrificed themselves for the sake of the *Shabbos*.

In the Footsteps of Moshe Rabbenu

When R' Avraham Abish was rabbi of Frankfurt-am-Main, a Jewish businessman began opening his store on *Shabbos*.

Frankfurt had always been strict in its observance of the seventh day. And the rabbi tried to meet with him to convince him to repent and not cause such a terrible breach in the wall of tradition. But he could not find the man. He never came to synagogue, not even during the Festivals. He was afraid to ask him to come lest the man refuse and thus shame the honor of the rabbinate.

But the wise rabbi found a way to get the Jew to come to him. He told one of the prominent members of the community, who happened to be a good customer of the businessman, to take a large order on credit. He was to evade payment of the goods even when the bill fell due. The man would surely demand his money, upon which the upright Jew would suggest that they go to R' Avraham Abish to settle the matter.

And so it was. The synagogue member bought a large amount of goods on credit and later refused to pay. The enraged seller had no choice but to agree to press his demands in front of the rabbi, R' Avraham Abish.

When the two appeared before the rabbi for their *din Torah*, the buyer hastened to pay up his debt. R' Avraham Abish then turned to the merchant and explained that this entire thing had been a ruse to get him to appear before him.

The man was stunned. He listened while the rabbi admonished him about the duty of every Jew to observe the Sabbath, which was the 'covenant sign' between *Hashem* and His people.

The rabbi's heartfelt words entered the businessman's heart. "I agree to what you say," he said emotionally, "but I wish to ask the rabbi a question. How did you permit yourself to use such a sly ruse and stage a *din Torah* for the sake of exhorting a Jew about the importance of *Shabbos*?"

"It is not only permitted," said R' Avraham Abish, "but a commandment and holy duty. I learned this lesson from Moshe *Rabbenu* of whom it is said, 'Moshe is true and his Torah is true.' Moshe said to his father-in-law that 'when they have any thing, they come to me' (*Shemos 18:16*). Understand this as if translated: "When they have any reason to come to me." In other words, when a rabbi wishes to speak to someone for any reason and does not find the opportunity to do so, he must do what Moshe suggested in the next verse, ' . . .and I judge between one man and his fellow.' This means that the rabbi must contrive to invite that man to a *din Torah* and seize that opportunity to do what Moshe did: 'And I make known the laws of G-d and His teachings'."

When the man heard this brilliant answer, he was appeased. He promised R' Avraham Abish that from then on, his store would be locked and bolted on *Shabbos* and *yom tov*. And so it was. Frankfurt-am-Main continued to be a fortress for the observance of *Shabbos*, as it had always been.

29 Adar

The new month is ushered in. This is two weeks before the Exodus of the Jews from Egypt. On this day, close to sunset, *Hashem* taught Moshe *Rabbenu* how to determine the new month by the new moon. This took place in 2448 (1312 B.C.E.). See Rashi to *Shemos* 12:2.

The Plot of the Baysusim

During the time of the *Beis Hamikdash* the new month was not established according to a calendar, as it is today, but by witnesses.

When people beheld the moon making its first appearance of the month on the eve of *rosh chodesh* they would come to the *Beis Hamikdash* in Jerusalem to testify before the court.

The Sages of the court would question the witnesses and when they found that two witnesses had identical evidence —

that they had spotted the moon at the same time, in the same place and with the same shape — they would usher in the new month.

The head of the *beis din* would announce aloud, "*Mekudash* — Sanctified!" and the people present at the time would repeat, "*Mekudash! Mekudash!*"

This was how the new moon was proclaimed. The day when this took place was *rosh chodesh* and special sacrifices were offered.

There was a time in history when evil men sought to mislead the courts and have *rosh chodesh* occur upon a different day. They wanted to begin counting the *omer* on a Sunday. Their leader, Baysus, rejected the oral tradition handed down at Mount Sinai and when the Torah said, 'You shall begin counting from the morrow of the *Shabbos*,' he took it literally. This was false and counter to our Sages' interpretation. Baysus misled a great many people. They left the ways of the Torah and later joined the Romans, enemies of the Jews, hoping thus to strike out at the traditional, Torah-true ranks.

In order to have the counting of the *omer* begin on a Sunday, they would hire false witnesses to say that they saw the new moon on Friday night. If the month of *Nisan* was proclaimed on *Shabbos*, the fifteenth would automatically fall on *Shabbos*, as well, and the *omer* would be sacrificed according to their plan, on Sunday.

The Baysusim hired two men, paying them two hundred *zuzim* apiece, a huge sum. The men had to appear before the court in Jerusalem and testify that they saw the new moon on Friday night.

The two men took their bribes and promised to fulfill their mission.

The Baysusim were certain that they could rely on those men, having paid them so generously. One of them was a genuine Baysosi, a man who believed as they did. He was fully prepared to utter the lie without batting an eyelash. But the other was a Jew who was true to his tradition; he, merely, pretended to agree.

When the two men reached Jerusalem, they went at once to the court to testify. They were separated so that their testimony could be verified. The first one to be questioned was the Baysusi. The Sages asked him the usual questions. He told them that he had seen the new moon at such an hour, in such a place and that it had had such a shape.

Then, the second witness was called in to describe what he had seen.

He said thus: "I saw it rising in Maaleh Adumim (a place not far from Jerusalem), crouching between two boulders. Its head looked like a calf's, its ears like a goat's, its horns like a deer's and its tail lay between its legs. I took a look at it and fell back in fright. And if you don't believe me," he added, "here are the two hundred *zuzim* which I was given for my testimony, tied securely in my robe."

The Sages asked him, "Who sent you here to testify?"

"The Baysusim offered to pay me and my partner, each, two hundred *zuzim* to come here and testify falsely. They wanted *Pesach* to fall on *Shabbos* and not on any other day. When I heard their offer I thought that I should come and warn you, rather than let someone else come and fool you!"

The Sages thanked him and said, "Keep the money for yourself. You are under no obligation to return it even though you tricked the Baysusim and failed to fulfill your mission. That money is their fine. They will receive a punishment of lashes, besides!"

After that incident, the Sages made a regulation that testimony for the viewing of the new moon would not be accepted from any random person, but only from reputable men who were known to be honest, trustworthy and faithful. (*Rosh Hashanah 22-23*)